Snowed in with the Firefighter

a Shadow Creek, Montana novel

Snowed in with the Firefighter

a Shadow Creek, Montana novel

VICTORIA JAMES

This book is a work of fiction. Names, characters, places, and incidents are the product of the author's imagination or are used fictitiously. Any resemblance to actual events, locales, or persons, living or dead, is coincidental.

Copyright © 2020 by Victoria James. All rights reserved, including the right to reproduce, distribute, or transmit in any form or by any means. For information regarding subsidiary rights, please contact the Publisher.

Entangled Publishing, LLC
10940 S Parker Rd
Suite 327
Parker, CO 80134
rights@entangledpublishing.com

Bliss is an imprint of Entangled Publishing, LLC.

Edited by Heather Howland
Cover design by Bree Archer
Cover photography by Georgijevic, standret, Karvas, and Marseas/Getty Images

Manufactured in the United States of America

First Edition November 2020

Chapter One

It was the cutest, most cheerful-looking little cabin Melody Mayberry had ever seen.

She hated it instantly.

It was exactly the opposite of how she was feeling right now. And, okay, maybe she didn't *hate* it. It was just so...*happy*, and she was the furthest she'd ever been from happy. Had she ever been happy? That was the question. Maybe she'd spent her life chasing someone else's version of happiness, and when that all came crashing down, she'd been left with nothing.

Which was why she was here, staring at a cabin, with no idea what she was supposed to do with her life now that her career at the hospital, the only thing she'd prided herself on, had just gone up in flames.

She clutched the steering wheel tightly even though she wasn't driving and the ignition was already off. Deep breaths. She needed to take deep breaths. Closing her eyes, she forced her grip to relax and counted to ten. When she opened her eyes again, it was with a determination to be positive. People were happy at Christmas, right? Or was that statistic that people were really depressed during the holidays?

Get it together, Melody.

She peered through the snowy windshield of her car again. The house in the middle-of-nowhere Montana was straight off the *Country Living* Instagram feed. It was just as adorable as her sister, Molly, and brother-in-law, Ben, who owned this red cabin. The front porch, with its perfectly stacked logs of wood and a stone chimney, which promised long nights with wine by a roaring fire, almost made her want to believe in the magic of a season that had lost its wonder these last few years.

Molly and Ben had probably enjoyed long nights together by the fire. Her youngest sister, Addie, and Addie's new husband Drew and his daughter had also probably enjoyed hot chocolate and marshmallows in front of the cozy fireplace.

She, on the other hand, would not be enjoying long nights or even short nights with anyone. That was fine. She'd never wanted a relationship anyway. There wasn't time for that. Especially not now. She was here to be *away* from people.

She glanced over at her phone as it vibrated on the passenger seat. *Are you there yet? Text when you're there.*

Sighing out loud in the car, she picked up her phone and texted Molly back. *Sitting in the driveway. This is the cutest-looking place ever. Thanks again for letting me stay here. See you soon, xo.*

She loved her sister and brother-in-law. Molly and Ben were even cuter than this cabin, actually. Molly was a doctor; Ben was a firefighter. They were…the perfect couple. She was the one with the problem, not them. And no one in her family knew just how badly she was struggling right now. She was a master at hiding her emotions, even from herself. They knew what had happened at the hospital, but she had reassured everyone she was fine and just needed a vacation because she never took them. All true. Except the part about being fine.

Maybe in her short career she'd been blessed. Or lucky. Maybe that was why she'd never had anything go really wrong during a delivery. She knew the statistics. She knew this happened. She had just never counted on how losing a baby during a delivery would feel, how it would make her question every single decision she'd made that night, how it would haunt her.

Or that she would never forgive herself.

But she was going to sort herself out here…in the middle of nowhere, hours away from Shadow Creek, in blissful solitude. Then, in one month, when Christmas and New Year's were over, she was going to go home, resign her role as an OB/GYN at the Shadow Creek Hospital, and go back to being her old self. Before her biggest screw-up and most devastating night of her career. Right.

She glanced over at her pile of comfort groceries and forced a smile. She could do this. She could take a whole month and not work. It had never been done in the history of Melody. Ever. Even as a child, she was always studying, always trying to get ahead and earn her mother's approval. But that's what growth was about, right?

She swallowed down the self-loathing as she remembered what an awful person she used to be. Maybe she deserved all this misery. It was the universe's way of telling her she'd never be like her amazing sisters. Her mom was really good at reminding her of the fact.

She buttoned up her coat and slipped on her gloves, pushing aside those thoughts. She was also going to work on her stress while she was here, starting with downloading a yoga app. Her muscles were so tight, they felt like they might snap in the cold.

As she opened the door, a gust of bitter wind hit her face along with a blast of icy snow. After gathering her purse, suitcase, giant bag of pity-party food, and extra-large fully loaded Luigi's pizza, she trudged up the walkway, barely managing to hold it all. She was grateful the porch light had been left on. She dumped everything—except the pizza, she was guarding that with her life—on the adorable front mat featuring a vintage red pickup truck with a Christmas tree sticking out of the back and a dog in the driver's seat. The scent of cedar from the fresh wreath on the red door teased her nose and almost made her wish she was happy for the holidays.

Finally finding the front door key they'd given her, she managed to juggle all her belongings over the threshold and into the semi-dark house.

She placed her bag of groceries on the large island with a *thud* and immediately tensed.

Movement sounded behind her.

She spun around just as a man's silhouette emerged from the dark hallway. Shrieking, she dropped the pizza and made for the door.

"Melody?"

She froze. *I know that voice...*

The light flicked on, and Ben's brother Finn stood there, wearing nothing but a pair of navy and white striped boxers and a frown. *Sensory overload.* She hadn't seen Finn in... forever. He had changed since she'd last seen him. He was thinner maybe, making every hard ounce of muscle more clearly defined. He also had a beard, and it seemed so strange on him...not that he didn't look good. He looked... scruffy, disheveled, in a way that was oddly appealing to her. Finn was a guy who'd always made her heart race, and that hadn't changed. His brown eyes weren't sparkling like she remembered, and his dark brown hair was longer.

He'd been through a hard year himself. After getting injured on the job as a firefighter, he'd been forced to take an indefinite leave of absence until he was fully healed. He'd been in the ICU for a long time, and for a while, no one knew if he'd pull through. Her heart squeezed as he walked forward, his limp obvious.

Ben and Finn had always been the kind of guys who would stand out in a crowd…or downtown Shadow Creek when she asked him to prom. She'd had *such* a huge crush on him, but there was no way a boy like Finn Matthews would ever ask her. So she decided to suck up the courage and ask him herself, if only to prove to her mom that she could find a date just as easily as Molly, her beautiful sister, who was already madly in love with Ben.

She'd never live down the humiliation of falling on her ass in front of him, her mother, and half the town when he turned her down outside of Luigi's Pizza in downtown Shadow Creek.

Ever since then, she'd gone out of her way to avoid him. He never mentioned it and was always overly polite to her— the kind of polite a person was when they felt bad for the other person. It didn't matter anymore anyway. They never would have worked out. She'd been ridiculous and insecure and desperate. She was an adult now. She only had half the issues she used to have.

"I, uh, wasn't expecting you," he said, glancing over her shoulder. "Are you by yourself or is the entire family going to burst through the door behind you?"

She was slightly relieved that he seemed to find "just her" more palatable than the entire crew. But why was he even here? "Just me. And pizza."

He ran a hand over his jaw, his eyes traveling from her to the box on the ground. "We need to save that pizza. I haven't had Luigi's in months."

Of course he was happier about the locally famous pizza than he was about her impromptu arrival. Maybe he really wasn't expecting her up here at all, and not just at this hour of the night. She certainly hadn't been expecting *him*. She crouched down and picked it up, placing the closed box on the counter. "Right. Well, help yourself. I'm pretty sure it's ruined."

"Uh, Luigi's is never ruined. I can peel the cheese off the lid if necessary."

He walked toward the kitchen, and her mouth went dry because, despite the limp, the beard, and the shaggy hair, Finn was still the most gorgeous thing she'd ever seen. The beard made him look serious. Like, so different from Ben's younger, easier-going, life-of-the-party brother. So different from the guy who had said no to taking her to prom. Not that she actually remembered that day or thought about it. Ever. Once in a while. Maybe a little more now that she'd moved back to Shadow Creek.

"Don't look at me like that. I'm not going to eat your entire pizza. Maybe just a slice. This extra-large size is hardly big enough to share."

She flushed and forced a laugh, like this was all normal and that the threat he posed to her pizza was why she'd been ogling him. "That's funny."

He blinked. "I wasn't joking."

He thought she was going to eat a fully loaded, party-sized pizza by herself. She had no idea what that said about either of them. "There's plenty. Trust me. Also…um, what are you doing up here? Mol made it sound like I'd have the place to myself."

Something flashed across his brown eyes. "Same here. I had no idea you were coming up. Molly and Ben were just here last weekend and didn't mention it," he said, crossing his arms over his chest, causing ripples of muscles to be highlighted. He was clearly comfortable standing in the middle of the room in only his underwear. She was the only one having issues with him standing there like that.

"It was sort of a last-minute decision." More like a last-minute plea for help because she'd basically been told to go on a vacation for a month by her boss. She just wasn't sure *how* to take a vacation. And vacation implied that she was supposed to enjoy herself, which she was definitely not good at. She hadn't been about to waste money on a trip somewhere just to not have fun, so when Molly offered this place, she'd readily agreed.

"Oh, well, uh, I can just stay out of your way," he said.

She shook her head. "No, no, that's okay. I'll sleep here tonight and then head back to Shadow Creek tomorrow." She would not subject another person to her junk food–infused pity party of misery.

He shrugged, and she forced herself to keep her eyes on his and not the muscles that moved. Clearly, she was nearing some kind of breaking point. One night sharing a cute cabin with Finn was fine. He couldn't possibly remember the time she'd asked him to prom. That was over ten years ago. She still remembered it like it was yesterday, unfortunately. He looked just as non-plussed by her now as he did then.

"All right, no big deal. There's like a thousand bedrooms here, so pick whichever one you want. Have a good night," he said, turning toward the hallway.

Her heart sank a little. It's not that she expected them to have a conversation or that he'd be happy she was here, but…their siblings were married and about to have a baby. They were practically family, and Finn talked to everyone. *Everyone* loved Finn.

She unloaded her groceries, a wave of sadness washing over her as he walked away. Was she lonely? She was never lonely. She didn't need people at all. She never had. Maybe it was all this holiday stuff and seeing both her sisters happily married. *So* happily married. And she was…nothing right now. "Sure, good night. I'll put the pizza leftovers in the fridge," she said, calling after him.

He paused and then turned around. She ignored the slight fluttering in her stomach. Maybe he'd stick around and talk. "Do you need help with your bags or anything?"

Her heart sank. He'd asked with the politeness that had been instilled in him and nothing more. Not an ounce of friendliness. He actually sounded even more miserable than her. She shook her head. "Nope. I'm good. Thanks."

He gave her a nod and proceeded to walk down the hall with that limp that reminded her that he was going through his own crap. The last update from Molly regarding his health was that it was still unknown if he'd be cleared to be a firefighter again, but that he was doing great otherwise. Maybe that's why he was still hiding out here. Her heart squeezed as she thought of how close he'd been to losing his life and his leg.

Taking a deep breath, she pulled off her coat and turned on the lamp beside the front door. She quickly surveyed the small cabin. If she were in the mood to appreciate anything, this would have been it. A floor-to-ceiling stone fireplace dominated the small area, and the red overstuffed sofas were cheerful and filled with various Christmas pillows. Candles were arranged on a tray on the ottoman coffee table, and Buffalo Plaid throw blankets sat on the armrests and in a basket beside the lone armchair. It was a spread straight from the Pottery Barn catalogue.

She let out a sigh and turned to the kitchen. White cabinets with mouldings and trim that gave it a farmhouse feel graced the other side of the space, and a small white table was tucked into a corner complete with a window seat and view of the front yard. It reeked of happy people. Molly and Ben were happy people. They deserved all of this.

Speaking of Molly and Ben, she pulled her phone out of

her purse and texted her sister. She couldn't get angry with her. She could never get angry with Molly because Melody had been a horrible sister, and she basically now had to spend the rest of her life making it up to her.

Just walked into the cabin. It's so cute. Thanks again for letting me stay here. Um, why is Finn here?

She put the phone down on the stone counter and proceeded to gather all the items that needed to go into the fridge. Opening the fridge, she was relieved to see that there was a jug of filtered water, jars of supplements and protein powder…and beer. No wonder Finn was so excited to see the pizza. She ran over to her phone when it vibrated on the counter a minute later.

Oh, glad you like it! I totally forgot to mention that Finn is staying there indefinitely. But don't worry, he's really great!

She chewed her lower lip, dying to call Molly out because there was no way that she would have forgotten to tell her that Finn was here. Leaning against the counter, she stared at the screen, wondering why her sister would have lied about this. It couldn't be because she was trying to set her up with him, could it? Molly wouldn't do that. And besides, she had never hinted that she was remotely interested in Finn. She'd never told her sisters about that prom invitation.

She didn't want to upset her, and Molly was almost eight months pregnant. The last thing she needed was stress. Ben was stressed enough for all of them. That was kind of cute. Really, the man was a dream.

"Ben claims he had no idea you were coming up here."

Melody jumped at the sound of Finn's voice again. She turned around to find him standing in front of the fridge, faintly disappointed he was now wearing a T-shirt and jeans. Ratty jeans. Worn T-shirt. Beard and shaggy hair. Who would have ever guessed this would be a look she'd find herself into? She straightened her shoulders, the realization that he'd texted Ben about her mildly alarming. He obviously wasn't happy she was here.

She shook her head. "Don't worry. Seriously. I'll be out of your hair tomorrow. It will be like I was never here. Then you can get back to your...manly retreat," she said, scrambling for words suddenly. She was never at a loss for words. But this last year had been a nightmare and had rattled her self-confidence more than she realized. Until it was too late.

He frowned at her. "You don't have to leave. I've been up here for months. I can leave tomorrow."

She shook her head. "No, no. Your problems are bigger than mine. You can hide."

He crossed his arms over his chest. "I'm not hiding. And I don't have big problems."

"No, no, of course not," she said, searching for a polite way to say that she knew he was hiding and that him not ever being able to return to work was a way bigger problem from her having to leave work for a month.

His frown was fierce even though it was on such a gorgeous face. "Does everyone think I'm hiding?"

She started shaking her head and then nodded. "Maybe. But that's okay. I've never been a fan of a family gossip. Not really gossip, even. More like concern. Everyone is *concerned* about you and why you're not taking the physical to see if you can go back to work."

He ran a hand over his jaw and mumbled something under his breath. "Fine. Thanks for the family intel. I think I'll get to bed."

"Wait. Finn. You stay here. I have friends in the city I can go stay with. Honestly, this rural Montana thing is getting old. Maybe I need to be in the city for Christmas."

"You can't miss the family's Christmas," he said.

She tucked a strand of hair behind her ear. "That was the plan."

He frowned. "Why?"

She shrugged and waved a hand. "It's not a big secret. I just want time away. Like you want time away."

"They aren't letting me have time away. I know Molly and Ben...and my mother. I know I'm not off the hook," he said with a hint of a smile.

"So, you're going back to Shadow Creek for Christmas?"

He let out a ragged sigh. "I guess. And the baby's due around that time so...I can't miss that."

She smiled faintly. "Right. I couldn't miss that, either, but technically the baby isn't due until mid-January. I'll be back by then," she said, her voice trailing off as she thought of what this baby meant for her sister, for Ben. This baby was desperately wanted, and even still, she knew that it would bring out deep wounds for her sister, and there was no way she could let her go through that without backup. She knew Ben would be there for her, but Melody and their youngest sister, Addie, would have to be on standby.

"My mother is betting on Christmas," he said.

She shook her head. "Too early. But anyway, I should get to bed," she said, glancing at her phone as it vibrated. There was a text from Addie. She reached out to surreptitiously inch it closer to her so she could read it.

I know I should have told you that Molly was trying to set you up with Finn, but I was sworn to secrecy! We love you guys, and it seemed like a great idea when we were sitting by the fire and I finished my second glass of wine. Now, not so much! Love you, have fun!

Melody closed her eyes. She knew it. Of course it would be Addie to fess up first. Addie was the softy sister. She had a big heart and had never gotten caught up in their mother pitting them against each other. Sadly, though, Melody knew it was because their mom had dismissed her. Molly and Melody were both academically driven, focused on the sciences and math. Addie had been a dreamer, a natural in the arts...which their mother cruelly deemed useless. She had also ridiculed poor Addie for not being as thin as she "should" be.

None of them had escaped that house without scars.

"Problems?"

She snapped her eyes open and shook her head, turning her phone screen-side down on the counter. "No. Nothing."

"You look like someone who just found out their sibling tried to set you up."

Her mouth dropped open. "You know?"

"This whole thing had Molly and Ben written all over it," he said in a grim voice.

She tried not to be insulted by *how* grim it sounded. "I don't know what they were thinking."

He ran a hand through his hair. "It's that thing that really happy people do when they're married and assume that everyone else needs to be married or with someone in order to be happy."

Finally, someone who understood the way she thought. "Addie is doing the same thing. Now they'll all have kids. Which means they'll think everyone need kids to be happy. It's obnoxious."

"Presumptuous."

"Irritating."

"Stupid."

She nodded, and neither of them said anything. She stood across from Finn, in the adorable, happy little cottage, and had never felt more alone or more miserable just talking about their siblings and how happy they all were. Maybe they were all right and she and Finn were wrong. After all, they were the only two who had shut themselves off from the world during the most wonderful time of year. "So...I'll just go to bed."

He gave her a nod. "Right. Me, too."

"See you in the morning. I'll let you know before I leave," she said, picking up her bag and wondering where the heck she was going to go tomorrow.

"Melody?"

She stopped at the end of the hall and turned around.

He stood there, the light behind him, highlighting all the contours of his large body, the sharp lines of his face, the fine lines around his once laughing brown eyes. "Or you can just stay. Here. I'm sure we won't get in each other's way. Plenty of room for both of us."

Melody blinked. Share a cabin with Finn? The hottest man she'd ever met, who also happened to be the guy who'd turned her down at prom, whose brother was married to her sister, and who her family was trying to set her up with? A mansion wouldn't be enough room for them, let alone this cozy cabin in the middle of nowhere.

She should absolutely turn down his offer.

Instead, she heard herself say, "Okay. I'll stay."

Chapter Two

Finn opened his eyes, disoriented for a moment, blinking and staring at the ceiling as the sound of a blender blasting from the kitchen continued. Everything was so wrong. He groaned when he rolled over in bed and glanced at the clock; it wasn't even five in the morning. Didn't Melody sleep?

Melody. His newest problem. It's not that he didn't like her. She was nice. Smart. Gorgeous. But all that was irrelevant because he wasn't ready to share this place with anyone. It always felt like there was something hanging between them. Or maybe he was imagining it. He still felt guilty about saying no to her prom invitation. Maybe she'd forgotten about it.

He would never forget the embarrassment on her face when she'd awkwardly asked him to take her to the prom. He'd felt like the biggest ass turning her down, but he'd known it had something to do with her mom. Marlene Mayberry, long-standing mayor of Shadow Creek, had almost destroyed Molly and Ben's relationship. She had cost them so many years. She had also cost her daughters a hell of a lot, too. Still, he regretted that he'd hurt Melody's feelings.

She was very different than her sister, Molly. He had known Molly for years, even after she'd skipped town and left his brother broken-hearted. There had been a warmth to her that had stood out and made him believe her, even when Ben hadn't. But they'd found their way back together a couple years ago, and he was happy for them.

But this time was supposed to be about himself. He knew this set-up was partially his fault. On Ben and Molly's visit last weekend, he'd played up how happy he was and how he was ready to get back to the real world. He'd even gone as far as saying he was ready to start dating because he was tired of their pity-filled stares. Clearly, they'd bought his act and had wasted no time.

He'd tossed and turned all night, unable to get comfortable. His injured leg had been throbbing, regardless of the different positions he'd tried, and now when he'd finally been resting comfortably, he was awoken like this. He wasn't thrilled about sharing the cabin with anyone, but he knew he should. It was generous enough of Molly and Ben to let him stay here while he worked on his recovery. They had a fully equipped gym in the basement, and that had been instrumental in him getting his strength back after the accident. A couple months of rehab in the hospital had gotten him back on his feet, but being out here in the middle of nowhere, with his own gym and nothing to concentrate on but his recovery, had given him back his strength.

He swore quietly as he tried to swing his leg over the side of the bed and sat up. His leg was always stiff, no matter how good of a day he was having. He imagined this was what it was like to be ninety. Wincing with pain, he slowly completed a few stretches that allowed him to walk without too much pain then forced himself to put on some shorts and a T-shirt before using the bathroom.

A few minutes later, he made his way into the kitchen.

Melody was leaning against the counter, drinking from a massive glass filled with green juice and staring at her phone. She hadn't noticed him yet, and something about her expression made him pause. She didn't have any makeup on, and she was wearing leggings and a baggy T-shirt. She looked…different. Younger, softer, almost vulnerable. Her long blonde hair was pulled up into a ponytail and highlighted her fine features and perfect skin. She had always been gorgeous, but this was different. She wasn't as polished and perfect.

He rolled his shoulders. No need to stand here gawking at her all day. "Morning," he said, walking into the kitchen.

She looked up, putting her phone on the island. "Good morning! I hope I didn't wake you," she said.

He shook his head and made a beeline for the coffeemaker. "No, no, I love waking up before five when I don't have to be at work."

She gasped. "Are you being sarcastic? Omigosh, I'm so sorry, Finn. I shut the hallway door to the bedrooms."

"It's fine. Really. I'm an early riser." He used to be, anyway. Now it just depended on what kind of a night he'd had. But she didn't need to know that. He hated sympathy. Or pity—that was the worst. As far as he was concerned, the accident was part of the risks in his job. It wasn't a big deal. He wasn't the first firefighter who'd been injured, and he wouldn't be the last. Ben had been, and their father had died on the job, so Finn wasn't about to complain about a leg that might never fully heal. Besides, the last week or so had him thinking of taking his life in a different direction. But it was too early to voice to anyone—hell, he had never even considered anything *other* than firefighting.

"I saved you some of my smoothie," she said, pointing to the Vitamix on the counter. Molly had somehow managed to get Ben to consume these green drinks as well, hence the

Vitamix. But they had never managed to convince him. He stuck to the powdered form of vegetables in the fridge.

He glanced at it as he made enough coffee for two. "Uh, thanks. What's in it?"

"Spinach, mango, blueberries, parsley, spirulina, turmeric, collagen, and water. Lots of really great anti-inflammatory ingredients and the collagen is great for bone health."

"You lost me at spinach," he said, pulling down a mug and praying for the coffee to brew as quickly as possible. He needed to head into the gym and stretch out his leg; it was killing him to stand in one spot.

She smiled. "That's okay, but you're really missing out. So, are you still okay with me staying here? Because I was thinking maybe this will work. I'll stay out of your way; I have a ton of reading I want to get to, and I'm really quiet. You won't even notice I'm here."

He poured himself a coffee and smiled, trying to relax and not think about the throbbing pain in his leg. "Quiet like the Vitamix?"

She grimaced. "Sorry."

He was being an ass. Maybe he was even being anti-social. He'd been away from people for too long. "Joking. Of course I don't mind. Would you like a coffee?"

She shook her head. "After I work out and shower."

Shit. He kept his expression neutral. "You're going to work out now?"

She nodded. "Is that okay? I like to get it over with in the morning. I need to change things up so I won't be using the treadmill. I'm going to try yoga again. Then I'm going to try meditating, also again."

He raised his eyebrows as he listened. She seemed almost nervous, and he had no idea why. She was normally so pulled together. "Again?"

She stared at him from over the rim of her glass. "I haven't been too successful in the past. I'm kind of high strung, and I don't think my muscles relax enough to actually stretch and bend. As for meditation, I have a really hard time shutting off from the world. My thoughts wander, jump to all the things I have to do in the day. Since I'm off work, this might be the time to try and see if I can do."

He leaned against the counter, putting his weight on his good leg. It was interesting to hear her talk about herself with that self-derision. He kind of felt bad that she thought of herself that way. He wanted to tell her that she wasn't high-strung. But that would be awkward. And maybe she was. What did he know? He cleared his throat. "I've never been much of a yoga or meditation person myself. But it's worth a try. Supposed to be good for you."

She nodded, her face relaxing, and finished the rest of her drink. "Yeah. We'll see. I'll head down there. If you want to use it first, though, I can always stay up here."

He shook his head. "No, go ahead. I'll just wait until you're done."

She grabbed her phone. "Okay. Thanks. Oh, and help yourself to the leftover pizza in the fridge."

Her ponytail swayed as she left the room, and he forced himself to turn away. He shouldn't be noticing her hair or eyes or the curves of her body. The last thing he needed was to be noticing her in any other way than a platonic relationship. Eyes, shiny hair, curves, perfect face, full mouth, all that was nothing he should notice. Or think about.

His phone vibrated on the counter, and he picked it up, already knowing it was Ben. *How was your first night with Melody?*

He gritted his teeth. Figures his brother would make a joke out of his misery. He typed back quickly. *I wasn't with her. We are in two separate bedrooms.*

I know. I just meant how was it?

There was no "it" to describe. She went to bed. I went to bed. Now she woke me up because you have a dumb Vitamix in the house and she made a smoothie before five in the morning. Now she's in the gym and I'm waiting to use it. Is that enough detail for you?

He only felt mildly bad as he waited for Ben's answer.

Great detail. I'll be sure to fill Molly in.

Glad I could help. Don't you have baby furniture to assemble or something?

Already done two months ago.

Of course it was. He couldn't even begrudge his brother. He and Molly deserved all the happiness and this baby. Between their mother, who basically told everyone who made eye contact with her that she was about to become a grandmother, and Ben, who sadly had started telling everyone he was about to become a father, things in Shadow Creek were getting a little too over the top. But he was happy for them. *Then go bring Molly some coffee or something.*

Done.

He frowned. *Go to work.*

It's my day off. Which reminds me, Mom is harassing me about Christmas. When are you coming back?

Ugh. He put the phone down on the island. They never gave up. If he had been on a vacation, Ben would have asked him when he was planning on getting his lazy ass back to work. But his brother hadn't asked him once when he was coming back or when he'd be ready to be evaluated. It pissed him off. Because that meant Ben didn't think he should come back. But he could. He didn't want Ben to write him off. It was still early days with an injury like this. He ignored his brother's question and stared out the window at the pristine white snow, the same view day after day.

He was going stir-crazy in this place. He had never been

in one place for so long. Melody here was definitely going to make his life a bit more complicated. It would mean he'd have to hide the way he was struggling because he didn't want her to report back to the family, and he certainly didn't want her pity. If there was one thing he'd learned this year—his family could not hide pity well. But she didn't strike him as the pity type. She did look like she was hiding something, though. As far as he knew, she was single, so it probably wasn't a bad break up or anything. It couldn't be career related because she was as brilliant as Molly was, and those two had achieved more than people twice their ages. It could be their mother—she was a disaster, and he only knew half the story there.

When he'd walked in the kitchen this morning, there had been a sadness on her face, as clear as the blue sky outside. So maybe he wasn't the only one running. Maybe that would make her stay less intrusive. They could just stay on different schedules and interact as little as possible.

He glanced over at the remaining green smoothie in the Vitamix and decided to pour himself a glass. It would be stupid to waste it. He could use all the energy he could get anyway. As soon as she was finished in the gym, he was going to prove to himself that he was getting better. He just needed to work harder, to rebuild the damaged muscle. In the meantime, he would research other opportunities on his own.

• • •

Melody scowled at the instructor's face on the Barre app as the woman gracefully and easily stretched her long legs in front of her and then lowered her upper body until she touched her toes. How the heck could she do that? The instructor folded her top half over her bottom half like a perfectly pressed sheet.

Melody gritted her teeth and paused the segment and attempted to do the same, except she only made it to her shins. This was ridiculous. She was in good shape. She ran. And she ran around the hospital, on her feet for hours a day. How hard was it to fold over like that? She tried again and swore when she felt something snap. She clutched her lower back. Clearly her muscles didn't work like that. Fine. That was fine. Baby steps. She would try again tomorrow. And then the next.

She rubbed her lower back and eyed the treadmill. Maybe she'd just stick with running. Running had always agreed with her. It was a perfectly acceptable way to relieve stress. Maybe yoga and all that stuff was just overrated. She could drink decaf tea if she needed to relax.

Or she could just not exercise at all…and just mope around on the house all day, avoiding Christmas movies. She sat up a little straighter and rolled her shoulders. She could drink coffee, put on a warm sweater, and pretend that she wasn't running away from life. She could eat all the comfort food she'd brought and not worry about achieving any kind of goals other than brushing her teeth and showering. Yes, she could totally run away from life.

Except life was upstairs—in very fine form, thanks to Finn. Staring at the treadmill, she went back and forth about exercising and realized this was the first time in her life where she was avoiding it. Normally, she used it as a way to stay strong and energetic in a demanding job or for stress relief. She didn't need that anymore. Who cared if she was strong and energetic? Stress? She had none now.

She stood and stared at the treadmill. She didn't want to go on it. She could hear her mother's voice telling her not to put on weight like Addie, telling her if she ever wanted to be as thin as Molly she'd have to put in the hard work. She crossed her arms and turned her head from the treadmill.

Brushing away the disappointment in herself and the guilt, she turned off the lights and headed back upstairs. It was okay to take a break from everything every once in a while.

"Finished already?" Finn said as she entered the great room. He was sitting at the island with his laptop open and drinking coffee.

She didn't want to tell him that she hadn't worked out at all. Normally, that would have sent her into a spiral of guilt and self-loathing. Melody didn't quit, and Melody didn't run away from hard things. Until now. She shrugged and made her way to the coffeemaker. "Just a bit under the weather today," she said, pouring a cup, keeping her back to Finn.

Finn was going to be another complication for her. He was chatty and pleasant—well, he was before, and she assumed that even if he wasn't the same now, he was probably more social than she was. She didn't feel like talking to anyone. She didn't want to answer why she hadn't worked out. She just didn't want to. She'd had to answer to her mother her entire life, to be told that no matter what she did, it wasn't good enough. She'd been set up to compete with Molly—only Molly had no idea. But their mother had pitted Melody against her, using Melody's desire to have her mother's affections as a way to fuel a one-sided competition.

But Melody had learned the truth two years ago and had been left reeling. Her entire life had been one big manipulation. She didn't even know who she would have been if she hadn't been forced in a certain direction. Would she have even been a doctor? Or had she really done all of this to please her mother? She had turned away so many opportunities for a social life, true friends, guys, everything because she had been so focused on her career goals—but she didn't know if it had just all been to prove to her mother that she was good enough. How could she have not seen that until two years ago, after reconnecting with her sisters?

Finn and his older brother were so close. He would never understand the kind of sister she'd been to Molly. Melody had been jealous and resentful of Molly. She'd let herself be manipulated by their mom, and when Molly needed her most, she hadn't been there. She would never forgive herself for that. He and Ben were well-rounded and perfect. It was hard to be around people this well-adjusted. She would make sure she didn't use the Vitamix until later in the morning, though. She'd felt really guilty when he'd walked in with circles under his eyes. He clearly hadn't slept enough.

"You okay?" Finn asked, his deep voice laced with worry as he shut the lid on his laptop and gave her his full attention.

She took a sip of coffee and avoided facing him. "Yeah. Just burned out. I figured there's no point in pushing myself. I'm supposed to be here to relax. I might just spend the day on the couch."

"Well, this is a good place to recharge. There is literally nothing around here for miles. No interruptions, no drop-in guests, no noise. It's perfect. Sometimes, I see deer. Most mornings, actually," he said.

She raised her eyebrows and glanced out the window. "That's a nice way to start the day. I could get used to that." With a smile, she turned back to him. "How will you ever go back?"

He shrugged and stood. "It won't be easy. But I guess I'll know when the time is right. I can't stay here forever. I'll have to get back to regular life. I'm not actually sure I'll be going back to Shadow Creek, though. I haven't exactly committed one way or the other."

She held onto the mug a little tighter, wanting to know more about his plans, because right now never going back sounded like the perfect plan. "Really? You would give it all up?"

His jaw clenched. "Some days, I don't think I have a

choice. I don't know if I'll ever be what I used to be. Other days, I think it will just take time and I need to learn how to be patient. But no matter what, if I go back to Shadow Creek, I'll have to face everyone at the fire station, and it's not something I'm prepared to do. Because if I'm not physically able, seeing everyone there will hurt like hell," he said, bracing his arms on the counter and looking out the window.

Her heart squeezed with sympathy. But she understood the pressure and the need to stay away. It dawned on her that he was much better at articulating his feelings than she was. He was also better at sharing. He and Ben came from a normal family, though. Their dad had been beloved by the town and his family, and he was good-natured and loving. Their mother, Marjorie, was a total sweetheart, and she knew both Finn and Ben adored her. There had been so many secrets and betrayal in her own family that she hadn't realized how dysfunctional they all were until she was an adult, and even then, she hadn't discovered the true extent of it.

She took another sip of her coffee, knowing she should say something. Her gaze trailed the strong lines of his body, and it was difficult to imagine that he might not be physically able to be a firefighter again. He was obviously in top shape, but she knew that the damage to his leg had been severe. Surgery could only do so much. "Time can do a lot, Finn. I know it's hard to be patient, but it might take a few more months to get you to where you need to be. You can't give up and think you'll stay at this point forever."

He hung his head. "I know. I also can't live in hope. I love having this time up here, away from all the pressure and just able to concentrate on getting strong again, but sometimes I think it's useless. Progress is so damn slow. What if it takes five years of just concentrating on myself? I can't do that. That's not a life, not the one I want. I haven't not worked for so long since I was in school. I don't really know how to take this much time off."

She could understand that. On so many levels. Her injuries weren't physical, they were emotional, and right now it felt like there was so much she needed to do to feel whole and confident again that it wasn't realistic. It would be easier to just quit. She finished her coffee and placed her mug in the dishwasher. "You and me both. I get it. This is the first vacation I've had in…like forever."

He turned around to face her, folding his arms across his wide chest and leaning against the counter. "What happened?"

She shut the dishwasher, avoiding his intense stare. She wasn't used to sharing her mistakes. Growing up with her mother and having her mother involved even when she was an adult meant never making mistakes like a normal human. As a child, any grade lower than a ninety was seen as failure and another indication of how she'd never be as brilliant as Molly. It's a wonder she, Molly, and Addie had ever reclaimed their friendship.

What had happened in that OR room would haunt her forever. She had never expected it to hurt so much, which was why she'd spent the last few days forcing it into a tiny box in the dark back corner of her brain. It was something she never wanted to unbox, let alone speak of to anyone. She had never been able to admit her mistakes to her mother without being ridiculed and belittled. Those memories had twisted her up so completely that she lived in constant fear of opening up. *Never let anyone see you fail* had been her MO since childhood. "Uh, just, work stuff. I think I've just been pushing for too long and it caught up with me."

If he knew she was lying—and she suspected he did—she was grateful that he didn't call her out on it. Especially since he'd been so open. Instead, he cleared his throat. "We all get that, I guess. I hope you're able to work out what you need to up here. I think I'll head down to the gym if you're sure you don't need it."

She shot him a smile, relieved that he'd dropped the subject and was now leaving. "Yeah. I'll try harder tomorrow," she said.

Something flashed across his blue eyes, and his face softened. "It's okay to not be a superstar every day," he said, his voice gentle and without judgment as he crossed the room.

She didn't respond as he left because she didn't know what to say. No one had ever told her that. *Do better, try harder* had been her life motto. With one sentence, he made her feel like it was okay to not always be the best.

She just wished that could be enough.

Chapter Three

Melody sat straight up in bed, her heart pounding, her brain still foggy with sleep. Something had woken her up. A bad dream? She had no memory of any kind of dream. She sat still and listened. Just as she was about to lay back down, she heard something akin to a moan or a cry.

Finn.

Her heart pounding, she scrambled out of bed. It was just after midnight. She crossed the room, opened her door, and stopped at the threshold to the hallway. All the lights were off in the house, and it was silent again. Maybe she'd been hearing things. Maybe she should just go back to bed. Finn was fine. Maybe he was working out or something. But after glancing in the direction of the darkened basement, she knew that wasn't the case.

This wasn't any of her business, and they barely knew each other. Part of sharing a house meant giving each other privacy. So, she should just turn around, shut her door, and crawl back into her nice, warm bed.

A low, deep moan, resonated through the hallway again,

and she knew she couldn't just ignore it and sleep peacefully. She hurried down the hall to Finn's room. The door was closed, and now it was quiet again. She couldn't just barge in there. But it had sounded like a painful moan. She placed her hand on the doorknob and waited for that sound again. But moments passed with only the sound of her heart beating like she was about to commit a crime.

It would be an invasion of privacy. *Go back to bed.* She turned around to do just that when a dreadful groan froze everything inside her and made her forget any reservations she had about walking into his room. She did knock, though. And wait. She tried to psyche herself up to walk in but felt like she'd be crossing into personal territory. But what if he was really hurt? Or what if he had the flu and his leg was preventing him from getting out of bed? *Just go in there. You're a doctor—he might need your help.*

Then Finn made some kind of noise that sent a shiver down her spine, and she opened the door, poking her head through. The room was dark, and only a faint ribbon of moonlight glowed through the window. She could make Finn's form out. He was lying in bed, on his back, his eyes shut. So maybe he *was* sick. "Finn?" she whispered, though her voice sounded loud to her ears in the quiet room.

No reply. Her heart pounding painfully in her chest, she slowly tiptoed across the room to get a better look. When she reached his side, she noticed the beads of sweat on the side of his face and forehead. His hand was clenched, and his eyes were squeezed shut. He made that awful moaning sound again, his legs kicking off the sheet. Her mouth went dry as he laid there with nothing but boxers on. But that jolt of awareness disappeared when she noticed the visible scars from the skin graft surgeries he'd underwent. Her heart squeezed and her throat closed up. He'd been so close to death. He'd been through so much, and he was alone, hiding here from everyone as he tried to heal.

"Finn," she said, though he didn't show any signs of hearing her. She could put a hand on his forehead, as a doctor, of course, just to see how hot he was. She wasn't even going to entertain the pun in her mind. Reaching out, she lightly placed a hand on his forehead, and he bolted upright with a blood-curdling roar. She screamed and jumped back, losing her balance and falling on her butt on the floor.

Finn put his head in his hands, his breath coming out in audible gasps.

She scrambled up. "I'm so sorry, Finn. I didn't mean to scare you," she said, standing beside the bed now, feeling stupid. Clearly, he wasn't ill because he was sitting upright. But he did look disoriented. Or sad. And if he'd been anyone else, she'd say he looked like he needed a hug. Obviously, she wouldn't. That would be…awkward. She wasn't sure she knew how to really give that kind of comfort to anyone. She'd probably be stiff, and she was pretty sure he wouldn't welcome that kind of affection. Way too awkward. They were friends. In-laws.

"What the hell?" He ran his hands through his hair and frowned at her.

She crossed her arms over her chest, suddenly self-conscious about the pajama T-shirt she was wearing without a bra. "I'm sorry. You were making all this noise, and it woke me up. You were…you didn't look well. I just touched your forehead to check your temperature. I thought you had the flu. And come to think of it, you should probably be thanking me, not frowning at me, because you're the one who woke me up and scared the crap out of me. I even fell on my butt." She backed up a step, wondering at what point in her life she'd developed the habit of talking too much when she was nervous.

He put his head in his hands and rubbed his eyes. He

didn't look like the Finn she knew, and the room felt small and stifling and way too personal for her comfort level. He also wasn't trying to apologize. The silence was intolerable. She made her way to the door, desperate to get out of there, to give him his privacy. He must be dying for her to leave. Who wanted to be caught in the middle of a complete loss of control? She wouldn't.

She heard a muffled curse and had almost reached the hallway when he called her. His voice was hoarse and raw, and something tugged at her heartstrings as she turned around.

"Sorry. I'm sorry, Melody. I'm not mad at you. Thank you for checking in on me. Do you, uh, want a drink?"

She slowly turned around. That moment, with Finn, sitting on the edge of the bed, his forearms on his thighs, his gaze on hers, she realized not only was he fighting his own demons, his own nightmares—he was doing it all alone. And that was uncomfortably familiar. He was trying to recover from trauma on the job, and in her own way, so was she. But he wasn't shutting her out like she shut out, well, everyone.

Even if he was uncomfortable, he wasn't turning away contact. He wasn't pushing her away; he was actually inviting her into his world. Her heart raced at the intimacy of the moment, of seeing him vulnerable and having him reach for company instead of solitude.

That's where they were very different.

Drinks would mean more sharing, more intimacy. This wasn't supposed to go this way. They were just supposed to be sharing a cabin for the holidays, not becoming…friends. Would they still be friends back in Shadow Creek? If they ever made it back to Shadow Creek. Then there was the whole prom date memory that always lingered in the back of her mind. It was something that reminded her of how insecure she used to be, how easily she had been able to toss her pride aside in order to make her mother happy. Finn had been there to witness all of it. But if she really thought about that moment, about that girl she was, she'd remember the sting of his rejection. She'd laid in bed that night, wondering if she'd been prettier like Molly, or thinner like Molly, or had perfect skin like Molly—all of the things their mother liked to point out—if he'd have said yes. None of that stuff mattered to her anymore, and she'd stopped that kind of superficial thinking, but that girl hid out sometimes, way down deep, wondering what he thought of her now.

Right now, this little place in the woods was the only place she could just *be*. She didn't want to leave anymore, and the idea of having a drink him with him was…better than being scared. There wasn't anyone else in her life right now that would understand the barriers she'd put up—except him. And maybe she did want to know him better. She always had. And up until now, she'd thought that was one-sided. "Uh, sure."

"I'll meet you in a minute," he said, standing and clutching the nightstand.

"Are you okay?" She resisted the urge to walk forward to help him, because she really didn't think he'd welcome that.

"Yes," he snapped.

She frowned even though he wasn't looking at her and turned to leave the room.

She heard a curse, then, "Sorry, Melody. I'm sorry."

"That's okay," she said, walking into the hallway. She understood pride. She was the epitome of proud, and she knew just how destructive of an emotion it could be. She hated to see that despite looking fit and strong, he was struggling—more than he was letting on. Probably more than he'd told his family, which was why he was still at this cabin instead of recovering in Shadow Creek.

She left the room quickly and walked into the kitchen. She'd pour some water for him. Her heart was still racing, and she had no idea what was wrong with her. Okay, maybe she did. It was almost the middle of the night, and she was going to be sharing a drink with the man she'd had a crush on most of her teen life after she'd walked in on a nightmare. That kind of interaction required more intricate social skills than she had. Would he want advice? Small talk? Or for her to help analyze his nightmare? She blanched at the thought. Maybe he just wanted a silent drinking partner. She could do that.

Just relax, Melody.

"Hey," he said, entering the room a few minutes later. She was torn between being disappointed and relieved when he walked in wearing a T-shirt and jeans.

"Hi. I thought you might want some water, too." She placed the two glasses on the coffee table.

"Thanks. Sorry for being a jerk back there." He walked over to the liquor cabinet in the corner. His voice still sounded husky and thick with sleep.

"Don't worry about it. I'm used to grumpy hospital patients. It takes a lot more than that to offend me."

He gave a short laugh and poured the drinks, his back still to her. "I can only imagine the people you must come across."

She smiled, her shoulders relaxing now. This wasn't so hard. "Usually they're pretty good."

The image of the last couple slid into her mind, and her chest squeezed painfully. They hadn't left the hospital smiling.

"Do you like brandy?" he asked, stopping her before she could spiral into guilt and memories. "That's all that's here."

She blinked a few times and focused on Finn. "Sure. I'll just have a small glass. I need to be up early."

"Big plans?"

"No, just another attempt at working out." She grimaced.

His lips twitched as he turned to her, holding two glasses of something. His limp was pronounced as he crossed the room. She tried to pretend she wasn't staring. "You know you don't have to keep the same hours when you're on vacation, right?"

She shrugged. "True. I've always been so afraid that if I actually really relaxed, I wouldn't have the self-discipline to go back to a rigorous schedule after." That probably sounded boring, but it was the truth. Not that what he thought of her mattered because Finn was just her sister's husband's brother.

"That's one way of looking at it, I guess. A vacation is supposed to leave you rested so that when you do go back, you can jump back into that routine, and if it's a job you love, you'll look forward to going back," he said, handing her a glass.

"Maybe I'll test out that theory. Thank you." Her fingers brushed against his, sending a spiral of awareness through her. She ignored it and walked over to the couch that faced the fireplace.

"It's never failed me, and I bet it would work for you. According to what everyone says, you're one of the best obstetricians around. A small town like ours is lucky to have you." He slowly lowered himself on the couch. She caught the wince he made before sitting.

So, he clearly hadn't heard what had happened. She was pretty sure that wouldn't be what people were saying about her anymore. Now it was probably about how she'd lose some patients or how they would be keeping a closer eye on her at the hospital. Or maybe that she'd been told to leave for a month.

But none of it compared to the feeling when she'd held that baby, when she'd looked into that mother's eyes or the father's eyes. She had never been so close to losing control in her entire professional career. Even her entire life. She'd always held it together. But something had changed in her that day. Something that made her very uncomfortable. She hadn't brought life into the world. She'd stared at death and couldn't stay professional. Tears had fallen from her eyes as she held their sweet baby, their dream, their love, and all she could ramble was how sorry she was. The nurses had taken over for her while she'd tried to pull herself back together.

She brushed aside those feelings and tried to give an appropriate answer that wouldn't reveal anything about what had happened. "It's a great hospital, and I'm thrilled I get to work with my sister and Addie's husband, Drew. I just really needed a break from it all." She didn't need to tell him that she wasn't actually planning on ever going back. No one needed to know that right now. She sat down opposite him, and that same feeling washed over her from the bedroom. This was intimate. Two people, sharing a drink in the middle of the night on a sofa. She pulled one of the cozy knit throw blankets onto her lap and leaned back.

She wanted to ask him what was wrong, if he'd been having a nightmare, but that would lead to more intimacy. Or he might just shut her down, not wanting to look vulnerable in front of her again. Or maybe she was just being ridiculous. Maybe she and Finn would come out of this whole thing as good friends. She could use some. And they would be tied together forever as family because of Molly and Ben. She hadn't spent any time in the last decade nurturing relationships of any kind.

There. That was it. She could be friends with the incredibly attractive man sitting beside her who had turned her down when she'd asked him to prom. This was a great idea. She curled her legs up under her and leaned against the pillows so she was facing him. His features hadn't relaxed, and she wondered if he was still in pain. "You okay?"

He gave her a nod and shifted, extending his injured leg

out in front of him. "Yeah. Sorry I woke you," he said, taking a drink.

She shrugged. "I'm a light sleeper. That's okay. Does this happen often?"

He gave her a nod and looked down, and she studied his profile. She had the sudden urge to reach out and run her fingertips over his beard, tracing his jaw. And she struggled to remember the way he looked clean-shaven, wanting more, to see more of him. His face had been an open book; he'd been free with smiles and laughter. So different from this Finn. "It's a recurring bad dream I've had since…after the accident."

"Oh," she said, wishing for something more eloquent. But she knew very little about his accident, except that he almost didn't make it. "I'm sorry," she added, feeling extra ill-equipped for this level of sharing.

He shrugged. "I'm sure they'll go away at some point. They are way less frequent than in the beginning. I thought it was the pain meds when they happened at the hospital, but they've lingered even though I never take anything heavier than the generic stuff now," he said, his voice thick before he finished off the rest of his drink.

She took a sip of her drink, trying not to let her sympathy for him show. "You look like you're improving, and the fact that you're not on any prescription painkillers is a great sign. I guess nightmares are a pretty normal reaction to the trauma you suffered."

He rubbed the back of his neck. "Yeah. I had therapy for a while, to get me past the worst of it. I hated it, though," he said with a short laugh.

She knew counseling was in her future, too—she just hadn't done it yet. The hospital had support available to all staff, and maybe when she went back, if she wasn't better, she would seek it out before returning to work at a different hospital. "I don't blame you. The thought of talking to someone about your darkest day sounds excruciating," she said, taking a sip of the smooth brandy.

He leaned his head back. "Yeah. Exactly. But to be completely honest, it wasn't as bad as I thought. And it did help. I guess time will fix the rest."

"It will," she said, trying to sound positive. She filed away what he'd said about therapy not being as bad as he thought.

"I guess I was naïve, but I thought once I recovered, everything would just go back to normal. I mean, I'm alive, I've been injured before, I've been in bad situations before, so why am I still having nightmares? This has taken me a hell of a lot longer to shake."

She huddled under the blanket. "Because you came so close to not making it," she said, softly.

He gave a stiff nod. "Yeah."

She took another sip and forced herself to break the wall between them. "What happened?"

His jaw clenched, and for a moment, she thought he was going to get up.

"Never mind. I don't know why I asked that. You don't have to talk about it if you don't want to. I'm sorry I asked. I don't mean to pry," she said, scrambling to take back her question when his features closed up.

He shook his head and finished his drink. "That's okay. I've relived it hundreds of times now anyway. It was a typical day until that point. It's weird because there wasn't a hint of something extra ominous that day. No sixth sense, which may sound silly, but my instincts have saved me before, and I thought they always would. But this time there was no warning, no moment that tipped me off. We were called to a three-alarm fire at a house on the outskirts of town. It was one of those old, three-story buildings that was used as a rooming house at one point and was in bad condition.

The fire was so extensive we were unable to conduct our customary primary search to see if anyone was inside." He stopped speaking abruptly and stood, walking back to the liquor cabinet and pouring himself another drink. Her heart was racing, wanting him to finish, but already aching for him because she knew how his story ended. It wasn't fair. He was so good at what he did, so young, so many years ahead of him.

He slowly walked back to join her on the couch, not making eye contact. His expression was strained, and his eyes were filled with a pain that she didn't know was from his physical state or the memories or both. Her heart squeezed, and a shiver stole through her body, despite being bundled up.

He grimaced as he sat back down. A part of her wanted to reach out and hold his hand. Or even snuggle into his side and offer him comfort. He seemed so alone, and Finn wasn't a man who was alone. He was the life of the party. He always had someone by his side—not her, but that was fine. There was always someone.

But here they were, and he was almost more of a loner now than she was. She shifted as she waited for him to continue his story. He rubbed the back of his neck and kept his head down. "I'm sorry, Melody. I...thought I was okay to talk about this. I can't."

Silence hung between them. She knew the rest. She knew how he'd broken one leg, damaged his spine, and had third-degree burns. She hadn't known about the nightmares or the fear that laced his voice. Finn and Ben had lost their father in the line of duty, and she witnessed the horror and fear that they all lived through when Finn was in the hospital. She had spoken with his mom, and she had been a complete wreck. She was the sweetest woman and tough, but not knowing if Finn was going to pull through had almost destroyed her. She'd aged so much since the accident.

She didn't know how Marjorie still managed to go on. How Molly was able to live with the fear of Ben's job every day. Sitting across from Finn gave her so much insight into who he was. Who all those firefighters were who risked their lives. He had been so carefree, so the opposite of this man. But this...sitting here with him made her really understand who he was.

"It's okay. I'm so sorry...I mean, I have no idea how you have that kind of courage to get out there and try and save people you don't even know. I'm so sorry you had to go through that. But you pulled through, you made it..." Her voice trailed off because she didn't know what else to say and her throat ached.

"I had no choice. I had to pull through. You do the same. You save people every day at the hospital," he said.

She shook her head, her stomach churning. "No, no, it's not the same because I'm not risking my life."

His head fell back, and he stared up at the ceiling for a moment. "I never thought of it like that before the accident. Well, I never thought about it too long. Dwell on the what-ifs for too long and you'll never walk out the front door in the morning. And it's not always like that. It's not always rushing into some burning building like in the movies. Hell, most of the time, we're running mundane calls...but all it takes is a day like that one to change everything. Some days all I want is to get back out there, and then some days, the ones that start out like this? I don't ever want to go back," he said harshly before standing.

"I wouldn't blame you. No one would. Maybe that's the hardest thing, knowing when walking away is the right thing to do," she said gently, standing because she didn't want to leave him alone. She hated that he was tortured. She had assumed Finn was invincible, that nothing could knock him down. This other side of him, this was someone no one saw, and he'd let her in. She didn't want him to push her away, and she didn't want them to go back to just being two people forced together and go back to hating the holidays.

He turned and faced her. "But walking away isn't who I am. It's pathetic. I need to find my way back because I can't just give up like this. It's letting fear win."

She reached out to grasp his hand, shocking herself. It was warm and large, and he didn't pull away. Something lit in his eyes, and his jaw clenched. She took a step closer to him. "Or is it finding another way? Maybe it's exploring different options. You don't have to do what you did before to be fulfilled. It's not quitting if it means protecting the life you have now. There is nothing wrong with doing what's best for you, Finn."

His thumb stroked hers, and her mouth went dry. His face was hard and unreadable, and if it hadn't been for the way he was holding onto her, she would have expected him to walk away.

"I have never thought of a life outside of firefighting," he said. "It was my dream. Ben's dream. Since we were old enough to know that's what our father did. We both looked up to him and knew we had to do this together."

She squeezed his hand. "Dreams can change. Life changes. And it's disappointing and it's not fair, but sometimes you just have to follow the path you're being led down."

"I don't want to be led down this path. I want to push through the old one. I want my body back. I want my job back. But I don't know how much longer I can keep trying." He scrubbed his free hand across his face then looked at her with dark, lost eyes. "Is this all pointless?"

She took a deep breath. "I don't know that, either. I guess you are right about not wanting to walk away because of fear. There has to be more. It has to be based on reality and not just your emotions. I know what it's like to want to walk away because of fear. The problem is that if this is your passion in life, if it's your calling and you let the fear win, you'll be miserable."

"Is that why you're not working? Are you not planning on going back to the hospital?"

Not going there. She went to drop her hand, but he held on. "How do you know that?"

He held her gaze. "It's a hunch. You're the workaholic. Worse than Molly was. You wouldn't just take a couple weeks off work. But there's more. You don't seem happy. Not like someone who is taking time off work. You're actually reminding me of myself," he said with a gentle smile.

She couldn't tell him. She wanted to. Finn was suddenly this safe person who would listen to her without judgment. She sensed that. But she couldn't share the way he did.

What had happened was buried so deep, under layers of shame and self-loathing. She knew she couldn't be a perfect doctor, but she tried so hard to be, and what had happened would stay with her forever. It's not that she was so cocky that she would be able to escape the stats of death, but she wasn't prepared for the emotional toll it had taken on her. She wasn't prepared to unleash her misery and shame on Finn. She couldn't even talk to Molly about it, because her sister was unknowingly wrapped up in all her insecurities.

Everything had come naturally to Molly. She'd been able to get ahead and skip grades in school without even trying. But that wasn't so for Melody. In order to keep their demanding mother happy, Melody had forsaken a life and buried herself in the books.

But it was never enough. She wasn't as kind as Addie, and she would never be as smart as Molly. She'd heard that over and over again from her mom, from herself. And when she'd lost her patient's baby…that day, her mother's face, her harsh words, had come back to haunt Melody. If she'd been smarter, more talented, she would have been able to save that baby. If she'd actually *cared*, that young mother would have gone home from the hospital with a baby in her arms instead of a broken heart and an empty womb.

She *did* care, and she *had* tried, but neither had been enough. What she had to offer would never be enough.

She tried to take an adequate breath, to push aside the rising panic filling her body, making her feel like she was close to drowning. She would never lose it in front of another person again. She would never let her guard down and be less than perfect. And she would try harder, no matter what she decided to do.

But oh, how she wanted to let go of her iron control just for one night. The idea of telling Finn what really happened beckoned like a fairy tale. She could just lean into him, maybe he'd wrap his arms around her, and he'd listen—without judgment. He would tell her he believed in her, that he believed her when she said she did everything she could. He would tell her she wasn't a sham, that her mother was the one who was wrong. That despite Melody having to work so hard to get where she was at, she was a great doctor. And then she could tell him how broken she was, how every night when she went to bed, she saw her patient's face when she told her the baby was stillborn.

She opened her mouth, her eyes not leaving his. She wanted to reach deep inside, pull up all the details, and tell him everything, but...what if he *didn't* say any of those things? What if he *did* think she'd blown it? She couldn't handle criticism from Finn. She liked him too much. She liked his company. She liked everything he represented. And maybe she just wanted to enjoy her time here.

Her mother was right. She *was* selfish.

She cleared her throat and tore her gaze from his and fixed it on his mouth. Wrong spot. It was a great mouth.

She looked at the picture of Molly and Ben on the fireplace mantel, in which they were laughing, on the beach. She had no idea what that kind of joy must feel like. Finn probably did. But she had turned people away like they were a dime a dozen, like there would be time later for friends.

That time never came.

Miserable over her own cowardice, she mumbled, "I was burned out. That's all."

He studied her, and she tensed, waiting for him to call her out. He absolutely should. Instead, he just gave her a slow nod. "We've all been there."

She broke his stare. Disappointment in herself flooded her body. Why couldn't she share the way he did?

"Are you okay?" Concern lined his deep voice, and he took a step closer to her. Normally, this would have sent her anxiety into high gear, but for once, someone else's presence had a different effect. She wanted to say she was always okay; she always found a way to be okay. But okay didn't feel good enough anymore, and she was barely able to make it to okay a month ago. Even striving for a mediocre personal life wasn't within her reach anymore.

She tried to brush off his concern like she brushed snow off the windshield. But she couldn't. Because he was standing there with worry in his eyes that did something to her on the inside. It…softened her. Made her want to lean into that strength he had. He'd told her what was stopping him, shown her his vulnerabilities, and she didn't think they made him any less amazing. In fact, his ability to talk to her made him *more* amazing in her eyes. She liked that he talked to her, confided in her. She wanted that. And for the first time, she wanted to believe someone when they said it would all be okay. Because this other way she was living? Constant work and constantly worried about appearances and keeping it all together was taking its toll.

She took a deep breath. "I don't know. There's more, but I can't bring myself to say it out loud. But I messed up. Badly. And I don't know how I'll ever be able to go back," she managed finally, suddenly feeling like she was stripping away a layer of herself. She'd barely revealed a thing, and she felt exposed.

His gaze went from her eyes to her lips and back up to her eyes again, leaving her exposed *and* breathless. He turned her hand over in his and covered her palm with his bigger one, lacing their fingers together. "Everyone makes mistakes. It's okay not be *okay*, Mel. It's okay not to be perfect all the time. No one is. And who really likes perfect people anyway? They're insufferable."

A small laugh escaped her mouth, and she leaned toward him, squeezing his hand, wanting more of what he was offering, wanting more of the matter-of-fact, laid-back attitude on life. More of the intimacy he offered just by holding her hand in both of his. Maybe it was the brandy, the warmth he exuded. "You think so?"

He smiled. "I know so. I also know you don't have to carry whatever it is alone. You can share the burden, let someone else in. Have you ever let anyone in?"

Had she? Not that she could remember.

She looked at their joined hands. Sharing with Finn meant crossing lines. They were connected through their siblings, and half of her issues were about family. She didn't know how much he knew through his brother, but she couldn't betray Molly like that. She sighed. "Thank you. But I should get back to bed."

His features closed up, and for a second, she contemplated taking it all back. Contemplated not being the disappointment she'd always been told she was.

He let her hand drop from between his. "Sure. I'm going to head down to the gym anyway. I need to do some stretching before I try and sleep again. Sorry to have woken you."

She stood perfectly still as he walked away, the distinct feeling of loss wafting over her. She had ruined something good. He had shared, and she had closed up. She'd given him a lame excuse. What was wrong with her?

Chapter Four

Melody groaned as her phone vibrated, and she glanced at the screen, knowing only a couple people who would call her at six in the morning, one of them being the most destructive person she'd ever met. Sure enough, her mother's face appeared, and she shut her eyes, letting it go to voicemail. She'd barely had any sleep because after her conversation with Finn, sleep had eluded her. She had replayed their conversation over and over again and wished she'd opened up to him.

When her phone rang again, she reluctantly opened her eyes. What if it was an emergency? She didn't want to deal with her at all but knew she had to or her mother would go and harass Molly and Addie, and that was the last thing her sisters deserved.

She grabbed the phone and sat up in bed. "Hi, Mom," she said, turning on her bedside lamp. The guest room was adorable, with its winter white bedding and white-washed furniture. She tried to focus on the décor instead of the voice on the other end of the line.

"Hello, Melody. I don't have long to chat, but I wanted the date of when you're coming back to Shadow Creek," she said.

Melody leaned back against the upholstered headboard, holding the phone to her ear. There was no way she'd ever press speaker when her mother was on the line and Finn was in the house. "I'm not sure yet. I told you I needed some time off. And why are you calling me so early in the morning?" No way was she letting her mother know that she was contemplating leaving Shadow Creek.

One thing at a time.

"I didn't realize that it was such a big deal for a mother to be concerned about her daughter. I'm only calling this early because I'm at the airport about to transfer flights, and I've been very worried about you. You have worked very hard to get where you are. People notice. *I* notice."

Melody closed her eyes and prayed for the line to disconnect. This was all the same old stuff. A few years ago, this would have had her packing her bags and racing back to work. Thankfully, she'd managed to figure out that her mom was a master manipulator and she'd been lied to for so long. "I'm not worried about how I look. I just need…time."

"I know you, Melody. You do care about how you look. You are too hard a worker not to care. Remember, you and I are the same. That's why you are my favorite daughter. I understand your need to succeed and be the best."

Favorite daughter. At one time, that would have been a compliment. It was now the gravest insult she could receive. "No, we're not the same at all. I thought we were at one point, or at least I believed we were because that's what you'd always told me. But then I found out the truth, and there is no way I'm like you. You lied to us about Molly. You said she was busy with school, and when she transferred colleges, you bragged about her drive and ambition. You let Ben believe she cheated on him and wanted nothing to do with him. Worse, you made Molly believe she was responsible for what that disgusting man did to her." Melody shuddered. When Molly finally told her and Addie what had happened, they'd all cried together for hours. "I can't get over that. Luckily, she gave us a second chance. We've spent the last couple years rebuilding our relationship. You have lost all our trust."

"That's a little harsh considering what I've done for you. You girls have twisted around everything I've done. All of it. Have any of you ever thought what it was like for me? I protected Molly."

Rage ripped through Melody, and she sat up straight. "We haven't twisted *anything*. You—"

Finn's footsteps approached, and she quickly shut off her lamp, her heart racing painfully fast in her chest. He hesitated outside her door, and she held her breath. She couldn't see him. A few moments later, she heard him walk away and then his door click shut a minute later.

She let out a relieved sigh, though him thinking she didn't want to talk to him was actually the last thing she wanted. She would have loved to have opened the door to him and spent the rest of the night talking to him.

"Melody—"

"No, no. I, uh, I have to go," she managed to choke out before ending the call and tossing her phone to the end of the bed. No more. She needed to not be such easy prey for her mother.

How much of life had she missed out on because of her mother, because of the insecurities she'd instilled in her, because of her need to be the best at everything? In the end, she still hadn't been able to escape death. But she'd been missing out on life, too. The man down the hall had escaped death, but he'd also lived. And he'd thrown her a lifeline that she'd stupidly let drift away on the current.

No more. Tomorrow she was going to start getting her life back together, even if it meant getting the ball rolling to leave Shadow Creek for good.

...

Finn emerged from the shower and dressed quickly. For the first time in a hell of a long time, he felt like he was getting his drive back. Or his love of life back. Life had always been an adventure for him—sports, firefighting, people, women. He'd loved all of it. He would wake up and hit the ground running. Since the accident, he hadn't had an inkling of that.

But after his intense nightmare and conversation with Melody, he'd felt...at peace. She'd been easy to talk to. Hell, he'd told her more than to anyone in the last year, and that was a shock to him. There had been something about talking to her, like she wasn't judging him; she wasn't forcing him into being the person everyone thought he was. He'd wanted to do the same for her, but she wasn't ready. He understood that better than anyone. He recognized a runner when he saw one.

The other thing that had become impossible to ignore was the pull he'd felt, the attraction. Yes, she was attractive, but it was so much more, and she was more than he'd originally thought. He'd opened up to her in a way he hadn't with anyone else after the accident. Maybe it was the cabin or that they'd somehow bonded in their need to get away from family and all the expectations.

Maybe the most shocking thing was he'd wanted to reach across the couch and pull her close to him. Or, once they were standing, draw her to him by the hand he shocked himself by holding. He wanted to know what pain she was hiding from all of them. Wanted to help her the way she'd inadvertently helped him.

The other thing was that, for a second, he could have sworn he saw that girl, the one who was so desperate to please, ask him to prom. He still felt shitty about saying no to her. He wanted to explain. And then he wanted to kiss her and tell her he'd never say no to her now. Obviously, he wasn't going to do that. That might have been something he'd do if their lives weren't so intertwined. They were practically family, so a casual relationship wasn't in the cards for them.

He pulled on his jeans and put on his T-shirt, pausing to look at his reflection in the mirror. He ran a hand through his wet hair, taking a moment to finger comb it, and stared at the beard. Everyone hated it. That kind of made him want to keep it on longer. But a part of him wanted to shave it off. At the time, he just didn't give a shit enough to shave; he had bigger problems. Then he'd kind of gotten used to it. New Finn, new face.

But now he was kind of backed into a corner because of his meddling but well-intentioned family. This was exactly why he'd stayed at this cabin. And yes, he was a meddler himself, and yes, when Molly had come back into his brother's life, he'd bugged the shit out of Ben. Frankly, Finn could take half the credit for getting those two back together. Now that they were the ones doing all the interfering, he didn't like it.

He'd woken up early and started researching an idea that he'd been toying with. It wasn't that he was being pessimistic, looking at other career options—he was being proactive. He had never not worked this long since he was in high school. He hated it. And what if he took the physical and failed and had no Plan B? Then he would have wasted a year and would still have to start over. He couldn't do that. It would kill his self-confidence.

Besides. Patience had never been his jam.

He knew the fire investigator in Shadow Creek very well. It was an option. His background would definitely help.

It was an area that had always interested him. It would still be tied to his profession. He could give him a call later and tell the man to keep it just between them and get some more information.

Ben would take this hard. Their mother would be thrilled. But this wasn't anyone's decision to make but his. He couldn't let anyone know that he was having second thoughts about even taking the physical because they would all think he was running. He wasn't. He knew in his gut that this was bigger than him. The gnawing feeling inside had been telling him that he might never recover enough to depend on his leg 100 percent of the time. In a job with life or death scenarios, anything less than 100 percent wasn't acceptable.

He rolled his shoulders and opened the door. He could already smell the coffee brewing. He was actually starting to like having someone in the house. Well, not someone. Melody.

He paused for a second as he entered the kitchen. Melody was standing there, staring out the window, her long hair hanging down her back, still slightly damp. He took in her curves appreciatively, and he remembered that spark that had lit inside him when she'd reached for his hand last night. It had been immediate and strong. And he'd taken full advantage of the comfort she provided.

When he'd come up from the gym, he could have sworn he'd heard her on the phone. He'd wanted to check in on her to make sure she was okay, but then the light had turned off and he wondered if she'd done it on purpose. It had been pretty late for a phone call, which led him to wrack his brain for any memory of Ben or Molly saying anything about Melody having a boyfriend. That thought hadn't even occurred to him. He just…didn't want her to have a boyfriend. That was irrational, really. Because they could never be anything more than what they were.

He was going to spend the morning researching the idea he'd been toying with the last couple of weeks. Hearing Melody also saying that he should think about a new career had given him extra incentive. He was just going to have to push aside his attraction to her and focus on his original plan of healing while exploring a new career opportunity. "Morning," he said.

She jumped slightly and turned around, giving him a bright smile. "Good morning. You look well rested," she said, grabbing two mugs from the cabinet.

"Yeah. I slept really well after. Thanks for not waking me up at five with the Vitamix," he said, joining her at the counter.

She poured their coffees. "I slept in, too. First time in forever," she said, handing him a mug.

"Thanks," he said, that spark he'd felt last night hitting him as her fingers brushed against his. "So, any news from Baby Watch?"

She laughed. "Nope. Actually, I haven't heard from any family in twelve hours, which is good. But I'm planning on letting them know I'm skipping Christmas."

So the call *wasn't* family. He tried not to let that bother him and leaned against the counter, putting most of his weight on his good leg. "Do you actually think they'll let you?"

She added cream to her cup and glanced up at him. "They'll have no choice. What are they going to do? Pack everyone and come up here for the holidays? There's no way they'd do that. Addie and Drew have Isabella, and Ben is way too nervous to come up here even if it's just for a few days. It would never happen. I'm safe."

"Don't you dare speak that into existence," he warned. "You know this family."

Their phones vibrated at the exact same time. Melody slowly put her mug down on the counter, and they maintained eye contact. Both their phones buzzing at the same time could only mean one thing: a text from family on that stupid family group text they thought would be so brilliant for Baby Watch.

She grabbed her phone. "We have to look in case it's baby news."

"It's not baby news. Ben would call. Like, serial dial," he said, making no move to grab his phone. He grew worried as her eyes widened and her hand flew to her chest.

"*'Good news, guys!'*" she read. "*'Because you're both up at the cabin, we all decided to bring Christmas to you! Ben and I, Marjorie, Addie, Drew, and Isabella are all coming. We'll be there by the afternoon on Christmas Eve. We'll bring the food; you guys do the decorating! Love you…'*" Melody put her phone down slowly, the color leaving her face.

Hell. Christmas with all of them? *Decorating?* He pointed at Melody with his coffee mug. "This is your fault. You can't just go around saying our worst nightmares out loud and expect them not to happen."

She gasped. "That's ridiculous. And not at all how the world works."

He shook his head. "You believe what you want. We're stuck either way. The worst part is they're all…" He grimaced. "Nice. Like, *too* nice. And over-the-top happy. And this is their cabin, so we can't even say no."

She groaned. "I know. They probably think they're doing us a favor. We have no choice. Other than just run away, which is still a possibility, but that's too obvious at this point. I guess we're doing Christmas and we have to fake being happy."

He frowned. "I'm happy."

She tilted her head, her eyes narrowing on him. "You're about as happy as I am."

"Fine. But I wouldn't say I'm *that* bad."

Her mouth dropped open. "What is that supposed to mean?"

He sipped his coffee slowly, deliberating whether or not he wanted to start an argument or end this conversation. If he ever hoped to get her to open up, an argument probably wasn't the way to go. "I'm just saying, you seem really unhappy, and it seems like I'm not the only one who thinks that. Everyone must. That's why they're coming up here. They probably already assumed you wouldn't go back for Christmas."

"How do you know this is about me? If I were them, I'd be more worried about the person who's been locked away up here for months," she said with a triumphant little smirk, which he found inexplicably adorable.

He grunted. "Well, when they get here, they'll see just how happy I am."

She shook her head and crossed the kitchen, grabbing a notepad and a bunch of different-colored pens from her purse. He straightened up, worried, as she started writing. "What is all that?"

"Planning. Faking happiness and Christmas cheer takes a lot of work. No one will believe us. No one will believe *you*, especially with that beard. So now we're going to start a list of things to decorate and get ready so no one thinks we're miserable. We have three days to get happy."

He walked over to the island. "Can't a man let his facial hair grow without constant commentary? This doesn't mean I'm miserable."

She gave him a side-eyed glance and continued with her notes. "You need to shave it off. They won't stop bothering you until you do."

He turned his attention to what she was writing. The page was divided into columns, and the heading for the first column was *Happy Decorations* in red ink, underlined a few times.

The next column was *Happy Food*.

He didn't even know what was happening anymore. "I

didn't know there was happy food."

She paused and gave him a pitiful glance. "Of course, because you're not *happy*. Hot chocolate, eggnog, gingerbread cookies…oh, marshmallows for the hot chocolate—happy people love adding those—and we should get some kind of pre-fab gingerbread house for Isabella."

"I think happy people make them from scratch," he said, just to bother her.

She shook her head, still writing. "We don't have time."

"None of that stuff is going to make people think we're happy," he said, pointing to the ridiculous list.

She put down her pen with a theatrical sigh and turned to him. "Do you have a better idea? I mean, the only thing I've heard out of you since we got the text is blaming me for bringing the family down onto us and your self-consciousness about your beard. We're stuck in this situation together, so it would be really nice to have some cooperation. Think outside the box. Like, look at this chart I'm making. I think we should make more coffee and brainstorm."

He was barely following her train of thought. "What? I'm not making a chart on how to be happy, Melody. I know how to be happy. I'm a very happy person. No color coding in the world is going to make me look happier," he snapped.

She gave him a side-eye and a smirk. "Sure. *So* happy."

He ran his hand over his beard and forced himself to not sound irritated. "Also, I'm not self-conscious about my beard."

She raised a brow and picked up a green pen. He had the uncontrollable urge to grab all the pens and throw them in the snow.

"You know what this is?" he asked, wondering how he hadn't seen this all along.

She finished her coffee and let the pen fall from her hands before crossing her arms over her chest and turning to him again. "Let's hear it. Hopefully, it involves shaving the beard."

He frowned and ignored that comment. "Well, you know how they're all sitting there plotting about us. Trying to set us up?"

She frowned. "No, I don't think so. I think they got the message. Nothing would ever happen between us."

He took a step closer to her, slightly irked that she felt that way. "Fine. Wishful thinking. Ben's trying to get me back because this is what I did when Molly moved to Shadow Creek."

Her mouth dropped open. "You set them up and meddled?"

He shrugged. "Yeah, it was pretty bad. I literally threw him under the bus. Our mother was coming out of surgery, and I told her they were engaged. I'm basically responsible for their entire relationship."

She tucked a strand of hair behind her ear. "I'm sure that's a gross exaggeration. But anyway…so? What does this have to do with us?"

"Ben and Molly must actually think they can do the same thing to us. What I did took talent. The whole idea is ridiculous. Way too much snooping in our lives. They won't let you go away for the holidays and run from whatever it is you're running from, I'm not allowed to grow facial hair without a doctor's note, and then they make it obvious they're trying to set us up. Clearly the only logical thing for us to do is actually pretend their dumb trick worked." He leaned back and grinned. "We pretend to be a couple for the holidays."

She choked on her coffee. "Are you kidding me?" she managed in a strangled voice, her eyes wide.

He wasn't sure whether he should laugh or be insulted. "Why would I lie about this? Think about it: we'll get the ultimate victory when Christmas is over, and we tell them it was all a joke. As if you and I would ever get together."

Her face turned red, and she started tapping one of those pens against the counter. "That actually sounds mean."

He frowned. "What? No. Ben and I have a long history of messing with each other. This one has gone too far. So, my ultimate victory will be letting him think he was right and then pulling the rug right out from under him."

"I didn't think you were that evil, Finn."

He crossed his arms over his chest. "That's not evil; that's just how we roll. So, let's pretend we're together and they were all so brilliant, they knew us better than we even know ourselves. We'll tell them on Christmas morning when everyone is opening gifts."

She made a scoffing noise. "Merry Christmas! Way better than having to continue pretending to be a couple."

He rolled his shoulders, a stiffness settling there, and tried to brush it off. "It'll be fun. It might give us something to laugh about. Remember, we need to laugh?"

Her green eyes sparkled, and she tilted her head to the side. "True. I just don't think they'll believe it. I've never wanted any kind of relationship…Molly and Addie know that. I've said so many times how I never want to be married or have kids. I mean, this is really far-fetched."

He tried to hide his surprise…and the irrational twinge of disappointment. "You don't want marriage or kids one day? Don't you bring kids into the world for a living?"

She shrugged. "Other people's kids. I don't want my own. I'm going to be the cool aunt, and I'm totally happy with that. You don't exactly strike me as the settle down with one-woman type. From what I've heard…"

He straightened his shoulders. "What? What have you heard?"

She tapped her finger on her chin. "Nothing."

"Well, for your information, I have no issues with

spending the rest of my life with one woman. And kids are definitely something I want. Lots of them."

She made a face. "Of course you do."

His eyes narrowed on her. "I'm not liking whatever it is you're implying."

"Look, let's stick to the topic at hand. Our fake relationship to ruin everyone's Christmas."

"We're not trying to ruin their Christmas." Not exactly. "But is that a yes?"

Her eyes narrowed. "Fine. Just one condition."

He gave her a nod, slightly worried.

"Shave the beard."

Chapter Five

The next morning, Finn stood in front of the bathroom mirror, holding his razor and staring at his shaving cream–covered face. Why the heck couldn't he shave it off?

"Are you shaving your beard without me?"

Finn groaned out loud, hoping Melody would hear that through the closed bathroom door. "I didn't realize part of the conditions involved you watching me."

"I thought it would be fun. There's nothing else to do around here. Like, literally nothing, and I don't want to have to do all the decorating myself. The only other thing to do is meditation or yoga, and I'm avoiding that."

He whipped the door open. He couldn't fault her there. They had spent the rest of the day yesterday hauling out boxes of decorations and making plans. And he'd tried not to be bothered by her no kids and no marriage revelation. That shouldn't affect him in the least, because when they left this cabin, she would just go back to being his brother's wife's sister, someone he'd see at the occasional holiday or birthday party. Melody not getting married was none of his business.

"Fine. Happy?"

She shot him a smile that affected him way too much. Speaking of too much, she looked way too good for this early in the morning. Her hair was pulled back in some kind of twisty mess on the nape of her neck with a few strands around her face. She was wearing a pink T-shirt with the word "Hustle" scrolled across the front and black leggings. No makeup. And she was the most gorgeous woman he'd ever seen. Especially with the teasing glint in her eyes. She perched on the bathtub ledge. "Very. I'll just sit here. You go ahead," she said, motioning with her hand for him to continue.

He sighed and leaned toward the mirror, razor in hand.

"Nervous?"

He swore under his breath as the blade nicked his skin. "Seriously? You have to pick that exact moment to ask me if I'm nervous?"

She cringed and handed him a towel. "Sorry."

He frowned at her reflection in the mirror. "Thanks."

Ten minutes later, he was staring at his face, feeling… unsettled. He looked the same. He knew he wasn't, but he did look like the old Finn. He made eye contact with Melody in the mirror, and her face turned bright red. Slowly turning around, he faced her. "There. Happy? Do I look like a happy person?"

Instead of giving him a snippy remark, which he was expecting—and looking forward to—her gaze drifted over his face for a moment before she stood. "Uh, not really. But, um, at least the beard is gone," she said softly, walking out of the room.

He frowned, following her. "What's wrong?"

She kept walking down the hall that led to the basement stairs. "Nothing. Time to do some meditation."

A rare moment of insecurity gripped him as he followed

her. Did she not think he looked good? Had he aged that much in a year? "You know, for all that drama about me shaving off my beard, I would have expected a little more of a reaction," he said once they reached the gym.

She stopped walking abruptly and spun around. He almost ran into her. She crossed her arms and looked up at him. "Are you actually fishing for a compliment?"

"No." Maybe. Which was even more puzzling to him. It's not that he wanted approval from anyone. Just her. What was even happening to him?

"Fine. Clearly, you are. You are as handsome as I remember Finn. I'm just… I think I liked the beard, too. I'm very torn. You can pull off both looks well," she said before turning around and walking into the gym.

He followed her in and sat down beside her on the mat, in front of the full-length mirror. "Mind if I join you?"

She stared down at her phone, tapping away. "Nope. Okay, I've got the app on. Time to meditate."

There was no way Mel was going to mediate, but he wasn't going to be the one to tell her that. Serene music filled the room, and soon Deepak Chopra's voice welcomed them and told them how to breathe and close their eyes. He almost laughed when he then told them they might not be able to make it through the full twenty minutes if they were beginners, because Melody was already frowning. "Talk about encouraging underachievement," Melody mumbled.

Finn choked out a laugh. "There isn't a performance review when you're done."

"I think I can handle meditating. How hard is this? All I have to do is close my eyes. See, eyes closed. I'll probably be so relaxed I'll fall asleep."

"Sure, you will."

A minute went by, and Finn was doing the whole slow, deep breathing thing, mostly just to prove to Melody that he could do this. He opened one eye and frowned when he noticed her eyes were squeezed shut. "You don't look very relaxed," he said.

She opened her eyes and frowned at him. "Why are you even looking at me?"

"Your breathing sounded weird. Choppy. This is how you're supposed to breathe," he said, demoing for her and trying to look like he gave a crap about all this stuff.

She made a strangled noise. "That's what I was doing. You totally pulled me out of my deep restful state," she said.

"Sorry, carry on," he said, shutting his eyes.

A minute went by, and this time when he opened his eyes, he caught Melody on her phone. "No phones!"

She jumped in her spot. "I needed to check something. Sorry. Never mind," she said, putting her phone back down and squeezing her eyes shut again.

"That's fine. I can get back into a tranquil state very quickly," he said, shutting his eyes and making a show of placing his hands on his thighs, his palms facing upward.

After a few minutes, he opened his eyes, shocked that Melody might actually be meditating. He frowned when he realized her head was in her hands. "Mel? You okay?" he said gently.

She threw her hands in the air. "I can't meditate! I just can't do this. My mind won't stop racing. I think of that to-do list, then where we're going to get all the supplies, the fact that we really should have already started decorating by now—"

"Whoa, easy there. Who cares if you can't meditate?"

Her mouth dropped open. "You can do it! All that deep, even breathing, the palms in the air, the way your shoulders were relaxed."

He laughed. And laughed. "That was all a show. I can't meditate, and frankly I'm fine with that. It's too boring. I'll learn when I'm retired or something," he said, stretching out his leg before standing.

"Are you kidding me?" she said, jumping up beside him.

He shook his head. "No, of course not. I was just trying to bug you. You shouldn't be so competitive," he said, ducking as she lunged for him.

And then she burst out laughing. Like a real, soul-filled laugh and it was the best thing he'd heard in months. "Well, I guess I deserved that. Let's ditch this and go hang some decorations," she said.

"You got it," he said, strangely looking forward to spending the entire day with her.

Two hours later, he was questioning his own judgment.

"The garland is lopsided, Finn," Melody said, her hands on her hips. She was worse than a drill sergeant. They had spent the last two hours hanging decorations he didn't even know Molly and Ben had. He shifted the garland to the side and kept his hand on it, waiting for her approval. She was slightly on the bossy side, but he wasn't surprised.

"Well?"

"Done! Perfect. Okay, let me check my list and see what's next," she said, marching over to the island to examine the color-coded list she kept adding to. He had even been able to withhold his eye roll when he noticed the color coding was all Christmas colors.

"I think it's actually time for a break," he said, glancing at the time. It was well into the afternoon, and he'd basically had enough Christmas decorating for a lifetime.

She frowned at him. "Uh, no. We have to finish."

"We still have tomorrow before they all swarm us."

She tapped her red marker against the notepad. "Let's go get a tree."

He frowned. "What? A tree?"

"We can't have Christmas without a tree. And Isabella will be here, too—she needs a tree. Where is Santa going to leave his gifts for her?"

"Well, after I inspect the chimney to make sure it's safe for Santa, he can just drop them and keep going," he said, crossing his arms.

Her mouth dropped open slightly. He'd been thinking about her mouth a little too frequently for platonic friends. "You were going to inspect it for Isabella?"

He gave her a nod, suddenly uncomfortable. "Kids seem to like that."

"Okay, I'll add that to the list of things to do when they get here," she said, giving him an odd look before ducking her head.

"Great. Let's have lunch."

"What? No. Get your coat on. We're going to head into that little town not far from here. Maybe they'll have a tree for sale. If not, we're going to have to chop one down."

"You mean, I'm going to have to chop one down," he said, grudgingly getting his jacket.

She lifted her chin. "I'm the surgeon—I cut things for a living."

He swallowed his laugh. "I'm not going to argue. My truck is in the garage. Have you been to that town?"

She shook her head. "No."

"Don't get your hopes up," he said, holding open the door.

Twenty minutes later, they were parked downtown, and he was once again trying to hold onto his laughter as Melody leaned forward and peered out the windshield. "This can't be it."

He leaned back in his seat and turned to her. "Yup. General store. Hardware store. Post office. Diner. What more could you need?"

She groaned. "A lot more. This makes Shadow Creek look like a bustling metropolis."

He reached for the door handle. "Let's start with the diner for lunch."

She scrunched up her nose. "I'm not really in the mood for bacon and eggs and home fries."

He scoffed. "Why? Are you ill?"

She crossed her arms over her chest and peered out her window in the direction of the diner, reluctantly admiring the multi-colored lights framing the large window. "No. I guess not."

"That's why you're not happy. A little bit of greasy spoon is what everyone needs."

She sighed and opened her door. "We'll see about that."

Chapter Six

Half an hour later, Melody squirted extra ketchup all over her home fries, wondering why she'd been missing out on life for so long. And really, why be so preoccupied with eating healthy when she really had no life? Why was she trying to preserve her arteries anyway? She jabbed a few potatoes onto her fork and watched as Finn polished off the last piece of bacon with a satisfied smile. "I was right," he said, basking in his triumph as he leaned back in the booth.

She nodded picking up her mug of coffee and trying not to stare at him. Obviously, she'd always known Finn was attractive, but witnessing him shave off the beard was something she hadn't braced herself for. He was even more beautiful than she remembered. She'd been tempted to run her hand over his smooth jaw, but that would never happen. "Fine. You were right. I should have never skipped diners. I also like this slightly ashy but fresh-tasting coffee," she added, taking a sip and forcing her thoughts off touching his face.

He chuckled. "It does have a unique flavor."

The diner was retro and exactly what she'd expected.

Except the Christmas decorations were more abundant than she'd imagined. Gold tinsel was strung along the walls and over the windows. A large tree was positioned next to the cash desk, and the multicolored lights cast a cheerful glow. "So where should we go after this?"

"Oh, you mean the hardware store or the general store?"

She smiled at him. Finn had this teasing nature that was almost infectious. His eyes sparkled, and his mouth always seemed ready to turn into a smile. She didn't think she'd had so much fun in a long time. Which was sad because all they'd done was put up decorations and eat at a small-town diner. "Right, I guess we have time for both. And then the tree, we still need to find a tree."

"You should try Sam's trees," the waitress said, placing their bill on the table.

"Sure, where's that?" Finn said, reaching for the bill. Melody reached out as well, and a back and forth ensued with the waitress sighing. She placed her hands on her hips and waited for them to finish. Melody reluctantly pulled her hand back when Finn put the bill in his back pocket.

"If you make a left at the post office and travel about a mile or so down the road, you'll see a red barn and a white house. That's Sam. Has the best Christmas trees around. He's also my brother," she said, her stern face almost cracking into a smile before turning around.

"That's perfect. Let's go. If you're paying for breakfast, I'll pay for the tree," she said as they stood.

"We can argue about it when we get to Sam's," Finn said as they weaved their way through the packed diner to the register.

A few minutes later, they wandered down the street to the general store. Snow was falling in gentle tufts, accumulating on the ground. "This is actually really cute," she whispered as they walked in.

"Not bad," Finn said as they surveyed the store from the entrance. There were only a handful of people, but for a general store, there seemed to be quite an assortment of goods and even a small produce section.

"Hi there, folks," a man with a white beard and a red shirt and suspenders said from behind a large, wooden counter.

"Hi," they both answered. Melody thought he was the sweetest-looking man, with his bright smile and sparkling blue eyes.

"Can I help you find anything?"

"We're just going to pick up a few groceries," Finn said, pulling out one of the small shopping carts by the door.

"Let me know if you need any help. I hope you beat the storm that's coming," he said, glancing out the window.

"We're in for a storm?" Melody asked.

"Several inches followed by ice. I sell salt if you need some," he said, pointing to the bags leaning beside the door.

"Okay, thanks," Finn said, and they walked down the aisle.

"Now we really need to hurry since we have to get over to Sam's to get that tree," Melody said, grabbing a carton of eggs from the dairy cooler.

"Yeah, and maybe some more food than we were planning. The storm might delay our family from making the drive up. Or, worse, make them stay longer," Finn said, adding a few cartons of eggnog and orange juice to the cart. They quickly made their way through the aisles, and as they approached the front of the store, something in the window display caught Melody's eye. Silver snowflakes were hung in the bay window and sparkled as the light hit them, and they swayed gently. Large boxes wrapped with red paper and tied with big green bows sat under a vintage-looking artificial tree. A red rocking chair sat beside the tree and the obviously fake cardboard chimney. But it was the array of snow globes lined up that caught Melody's attention. From where she was standing, one of them reminded her of a long-forgotten until now snow globe.

"Here, you finish the shopping. I need to go check something out," she said to Finn, leaving him with the shopping cart and walking to the display.

Her heart beat rapidly as memories tumbled through her mind like falling snow. She wasn't sure she wanted to really reach for them or let them melt away again. But she kept walking, unable to leave them. A shiver stole through her as she reached the window display and focused on the snow globe with the red base. It was the same one. The one from her childhood.

Inside the globe, just as she remembered, was a white clapboard house with a white picket fence and a snowman outside. Wreaths were hung in the windows, and garland lined the fence. She already knew that if she shook it, white and gold snow would sprinkle over the idyllic scene. How could this old snow globe be here, in this random shop in this town she didn't even know existed?

"Those are my old collection of snow globes. Used to collect them for my kids when they were little. Now they're all gone, and I like to put them out for the kids who come in," the man said from behind the counter.

Melody glanced over at him, caught between her memories and the present. Glancing over her shoulder to make sure Finn wasn't around, she turned to the man. "May I pick it up?"

"Of course! Give it a good shake, too," he said. The kindness in his gravely voice almost made her feel better as she reached out to grasp the globe.

She did as he suggested and gave it a good hard shake, and suddenly, she was eight years old, sitting on the sidelines watching as Molly did the same. Christmas morning at their house had been filled with presents given based on merits and manipulations. Molly had skipped a grade that year, and their mother had rewarded her with bucketloads of gifts; some were even from Santa, who had heard how smart she was. Melody and Addie had sat across from Molly, watching as she opened endless gifts while they only had one each.

Melody had worked so hard that year at school, every year, but she was never as smart as Molly. When Molly opened up her last gift, Melody gasped at the sight of the most gorgeous snow globe. Melody had asked Santa for a snow globe, but Molly hadn't. Molly shook it and held it up for them to see. She wasn't showing off; she just loved it as much as Melody did. Molly never showed off or tried to get their mother's favor. She had even looked uncomfortable with all the gifts she'd received, knowing it wasn't right but unable to say anything because no one wanted their mother mad at them. Their father had been at work, conveniently. Melody knew now as an adult that he had intentionally spent so much time away from home because her mother was unbearable. He couldn't stick up for himself or his daughters, so he just made himself absent.

"Well, Adelaide and Melody, if the two of you want gifts like this next year, you're going to just have to work harder. Even Santa had heard how smart and ambitious Molly is, all the way in the North Pole," their mother had said, standing over them as they looked at Molly's new toys and clothes.

Molly's face had turned red, and she frowned, holding the globe. When their mother left the room to make breakfast, Melody asked to see the globe. Of course, Molly handed it over right away. Jealousy and insecurity had consumed Melody, and she'd purposely let the globe "slip" from her fingers and onto the floor, the glass shattering, the water and snow and all the happy people spilling out, their magic destroyed.

Melody cried as soon as it happened, hating herself, guilt consuming her. But the worst was when Molly came over and gave her a hug and told her how sad she was—because she'd planned on giving the globe to Melody. She had planned on secretly sharing her gifts with Melody and Addie.

Then their mother charged back into the room and delivered a blistering lecture to Melody and told her that she'd have to save up with her allowance money and pay Molly the cost of the snow globe and clean up the mess.

Molly and Addie and Melody cleaned up the mess, and even though Molly wasn't mad at Melody, thinking it had been an accident, Melody couldn't look her sister in the eye for the rest of the day. She carried that secret around as a reminder of who she was and who she never wanted to be again. Now, Melody knew that their mother had manipulated all of them for years, and instead of trying to make them close sisters, she'd pitted them against each other. So much so that they had all distanced themselves and had gone in different directions, only keeping in touch casually. The last two years had changed everything for them, though. All their secrets and hurts had come out into the open, and nothing was going to stop them from remaining close.

But Melody hadn't told Molly about the snow globe incident.

"Are you buying that? We should really get going."

Melody jumped at the sound of Finn beside her. She avoided looking at him as she placed the snow globe back on the display, feeling shaky and sweaty. "Uh, no. Not for sale. It just caught my eye," she said, backing away.

Finn pointed to the giant bag of oranges in the full cart. "I thought you'd want to add some fruit. I think happy people eat fruit."

She was relieved for the change of topic. "Right. Because they like their lives and don't want scurvy," she murmured, trying to be funny, trying and failing to shake off those childhood memories.

He chuckled as they walked over to the register and started lining up their items on the counter.

"Did you get everything we needed?" she asked, helping him unload the cart. She needed to forget the snow globe and move on. There was nothing she could do about it anyway. It would be ridiculous to bring up to Molly at this point in their lives. But the guilt was still there, reminding her that she'd never been good enough, and not just in the ways her mother believed.

"Yup," he said.

The man carefully added the items to paper bags. "Glad you kids were able to find everything."

"You have a great store," Melody said.

"Well, thank you. You be careful out there. Those country roads don't get plowed fast enough."

"Will do," Finn said, glancing out the window.

Once they had paid, they thanked him and made their way outside. The weather had definitely changed since they first entered. What had been gentle snowfall half an hour ago had now turned to heavy snow and wind. "This is awful," Melody said as they hustled over to Finn's truck.

"It is. We better hurry if we're going to make it to Sam's." He placed the last bag in the backseat and groaned. "Shoot. I forgot to get bacon. Ben can eat a whole pack by himself. He's totally getting a middle-aged paunch. I'll be right back," he said, running off before she could answer.

She stifled her laugh at the middle-aged paunch remark. Ben was barely two years older than Finn, and he was just as fit as always.

A few minutes later, he opened the door and tossed his bag in the back. "Done. Let's go." They drove in silence, and what should have been a five-minute drive took nearly fifteen.

"There's the sign," Melody pointed out, relieved.

"Great." He slowed down to make the turn on the slippery roads. The parking lot was deserted, and Finn pulled up right in front.

Finn turned off the ignition. "I guess we're the only people stupid enough to be out in this weather."

"This is what happy people do," she said, shooting him a glance.

"This is why happiness is highly overrated. Let's make it fast."

Melody met him outside the truck and eyed the rows of trees. "This looks promising."

A man wearing a lumberjack jacket and matching fur-lined hat emerged from a little red house and made his way over to them. "Surprised to see anyone out here in this weather!"

Finn nodded. "Yeah. We really need a tree. We'll be quick and then be on our way. Our place isn't too far from here."

The man—Sam, she assumed—spread his arm in the direction of the Christmas trees. "Okay, have a look around. Once you've decided on one, I'll load it into your truck."

"Sounds good," Finn said as they made their way through the aisles. Luckily, the trees helped shield them from some of the snow and wind.

Melody made her way up and down the rows of trees, losing Finn somewhere along the way. Though she really didn't want it, a memory pulled at her until she couldn't ignore it. Standing still in between two large Balsam fir trees, she could see herself walking through the Christmas tree farm with her mother. Melody had proudly brought home an A+ on a project about the various Christmas tree farms in Montana. Her mother had promised that she would get to pick out the family tree this year. But then Molly had come home with an A+ on her science test, and since science was a more important subject according to her mother, Molly was allowed to pick the family tree. It wasn't Molly's fault; she hadn't even known.

Melody pleaded with her mother to get the large, fragrant Balsam fir, but her mother refused and told her that if her grades were as good as Molly's and if she could actually manage to skip a grade like Molly, then maybe next year she could pick the tree. But that never happened because there was always a reason she wasn't good enough.

Melody took off her glove and ran her fingers over the needles, the wind carrying the fragrance to her nose. She never bothered with a Christmas tree as an adult.

"Oh no, not a Balsam fir," Finn said, frowning as he approached.

She put her glove back on and stood in front of the tree she was determined to get. "What? These are the best. We're getting this one."

His lips twitched, and she wondered if he was purposely trying to irritate her. "Too perfect. The shape. The smell. No one likes a show-off tree."

Her eyes widened. "That's ridiculous."

He swiped his hand over the branches, and they sprung back to life. "See, it's trying too hard."

She reached her hand inside to grasp the trunk. "Maybe it's trying too hard because no one appreciates it. Maybe if you'd give it a chance, you'd see it's a really good tree deep down."

He studied her, and heat infused her body, despite the cold. What was wrong with her? Why was she making a big deal about this tree and making it personal? About *her*?

She swallowed hard as he took a step closer to her, something akin to either pity or sympathy in those deep green eyes of his. It reminded her of the ill-fated prom invitation.

"Maybe it doesn't need to try hard. Maybe the tree is perfect the way it is."

Her mouth dropped open, and the unmistakable twinge of desire swirled through her. His voice was deep and husky, and his eyes went from hers to her mouth. For a second, she let herself imagine what it would be like to kiss Finn. And she wanted to, she realized, more than to anyone. But it would be a pity kiss on his part. Because he thought she had issues because she'd just compared herself to a Christmas tree.

She tried to give him a fun, flirty smile but had no idea if she pulled it off. "As your girlfriend, I insist on getting this tree. I would think you'd want to be nice and make me happy. We're *happy* people, remember?" Her voice sounded strangled, and she backed up a step, right into the tree. "I'll help you bring this tree to the front."

He shook his head and shoved his hand into the branches right beside her face and grasped the trunk. "As your *boyfriend*, *I'm* getting this tree and hauling it to the front."

She couldn't let him do that with his leg. "I don't date show-offs. I'll help." She tried to swat his hand away from the trunk. It didn't budge.

"As your *boyfriend*, I'd like to do this," he said, yanking the tree toward him, which in turn brought her much, much closer to him.

They stared at each other, their breaths swirling together in the cold air. Melody searched for something, anything, to break the spell between them. If she didn't, she'd kiss the man right there on the spot, and that would be very, very bad.

"As a *doctor*, I do not advise you to do that on your own," she managed on a half whisper, half croak.

His expression shuttered, all the heat she'd swore had been pooling in his eyes extinguished in a second. "Well, you're not my doctor. Last time I checked, you were an OB/GYN, and I'm pretty sure I can't have babies, so you're out of luck."

He wrestled the tree out from behind her and started off toward the barn. She trailed behind him, kicking herself. She had to bring up his injury?

"Hey!"

They both stopped abruptly as Sam came marching over to them. "Hey, I thought I told you kids to give me a call. No unqualified people are allowed to handle the trees. I'll get this tree ready to take home."

Finn handed over the tree. Sam was frowning at them. "Sorry, Sam. Melody here was insistent that we bring the tree to you. I was trying to tell her that's not what you said to do."

Melody gave Finn a shove, but he ignored her.

"Well, see that you move back a bit. In fact, why don't you two go wait up front for me?"

"I'll make sure we stay out of trouble," Finn said, a smile lining his voice as they walked to the cash.

"Really nice of you to throw me under the bus, Finn," she said, hopping on one foot then the other in an effort to stay warm as they waited for Sam. The wind felt like it was coming from all directions, sending icy snow swirling around them.

"After your jab about my leg, you had it coming." She opened her mouth to apologize, but he just raised his hand. "*And* you got your tree, so being thrown under the bus to save our reputation was a small price to pay." He glanced over his shoulder. "Sam is coming, so don't do anything to piss him off or we might not get that tree."

Sam leaned the tree against the side of the fence and gave them a price that seemed pretty steep in Melody's opinion. Judging by Finn's long stare as he pulled his wallet out, she wasn't the only one who thought so.

"I'll pay for half," Melody said, reaching for her wallet.

"Don't worry about it. I've got it. I'm a nice boyfriend

who likes to buy things," he said.

"No, I'll pay. You haven't worked in a year," she said, cringing as the words came out of her mouth. How insensitive could one person be in a single trip to a Christmas tree lot?

Sam made a *tsking* sound. She didn't even dare look up at Finn.

"I've got it," Finn said again as he shoved a few bills at Sam.

"I could use some help around the farm if you're looking for work, son," Sam said.

Melody wanted to run and hide in the trees. Maybe this was why she didn't have friends. Maybe it wasn't that she wasn't making them—maybe no one actually wanted to be around her. Did she blurt out the truth all the time? No one actually wanted to hear the truth if it wasn't good.

Finn's hard jaw clenched, and she wasn't sure he was going to answer. Then he cleared his throat. "Thanks for the offer, Sam. I'll be going back to work soon. I have a job waiting for me. I just needed some time off."

Sam reached for the tree and threw it over his shoulder like a sack of potatoes. Melody followed, feeling awful that Finn was now in a position to explain himself. "Well, see you don't take too much time off. Sometimes it's hard to get back into things when you're not used to working every day."

"I've been keeping myself busy," he said, his profile stony.

Her stomach churned. Of course, he was angry. She'd pointed out his leg in a moment of desperation and then pointed out his lack of employment in front of another man. Melody squinted against the snow blowing in her face and desperately thought of something to say that would take the attention off Finn. "Thanks for getting this tree, Finn. It's perfect."

Not good enough. He glanced over at her and didn't look remotely interested in what she had to say.

"There you go, kids. Remember I've got that job opening if you ever need it," Sam said, slapping Finn on the shoulder.

Finn climbed into the driver's seat. "Thanks, Sam."

Melody scrambled into the passenger side, somewhat worried he'd just drive away. Moments later, he was easing the truck onto the snow- and ice-covered roads. Normally, she would just sit and be quiet because she didn't really know how to apologize. That was another weakness in their house. But as she glanced over at Finn, at the hard lines of his beautiful face, her heart kind of broke, and her insecurities took a backseat to his injured pride. "Sorry," she said softly, hoping he could hear her above the heat blasting from the vents and the ice tapping against the windshield.

He stared straight ahead at the road. "For what?"

"Well...it sounded like I was saying that you didn't want to work or that...well, I'm just sorry that I said anything at all."

There was a long pause. At least a minute ticked by, and Finn didn't say a thing. "This year knocked me down hard. Sometimes when it feels like I'm just getting my shit together, I'm reminded of everything I've lost. Of the guy I used to be. I'm not a guy who just sits around and mooches off family."

Melody wanted to pitch herself out of the car and into one of the snow-covered ditches. His deep voice sounded tortured and gruff. This was all her fault. It was so much more than pride or ego. She'd inadvertently hit a nerve. But he'd been honest about what he was feeling. And she owed him the same, even if it made her so uncomfortable. She couldn't have him sitting there thinking that he was any less than the man he was before the accident. More than anything, she wanted to reach across the seat and place her hand on his thigh or his arm, but she didn't know if he'd welcome her touch now. He was the first person she wanted to be completely honest with, and now she'd ruined this friendship they were building.

"Of course you're not. No one thinks of you like that. You needed to take a year off. You had no choice. I'm sorry, Finn. Sometimes…I don't know. I say things without thinking or realizing how hurtful it can sound."

"It's okay."

She chewed her bottom lip and looked away from his hard profile. It wasn't okay. People didn't just forgive like that. Every time she had screwed up, the ramifications had been deep and harsh. This was why she stayed away from people. She said the wrong things. She disappointed people. She placed her elbow on the window jam and stared at the swirling snow around them, wishing there was something she could say that would make everything go back to the way it was before her dumb comments.

"Hey." His deep voice was gentle now, and he reached out to grab her hand, sending a ripple of warmth through her. He'd reached out to touch her. She had wanted to do that but couldn't. "I'm not mad at you. I know you didn't mean anything by it."

He glanced over at her quickly before slipping his hand from hers and turning his eyes back to the road. He wasn't mad. Just like that. It was hard to believe. "Really?"

"Why do you sound so surprised?"

She wanted to make a flippant remark, but his honesty was still ringing in her ears, and she didn't want to cover up the truth. She wanted to give him what he'd given her. "I've… messed up a lot in my life, and forgiveness wasn't something I was given. And when it was…by Molly…I had a hard time forgiving myself. Or really believing that things could be okay again."

Her hands were sweaty, and she clasped them together. Telling the truth about herself and highlighting all her faults was not exactly an easy thing to do. Especially when the man sitting beside her was beginning to mean so much to her.

"I don't hold grudges, Mel. Life is too short. People screw up. Everyone does. Don't make this bigger than it needs to be. Hey, if it weren't for you, I wouldn't have had an offer to be Sam's assistant at the tree lot," he said, giving her a half smile that filled her with a relief and comfort she'd never really known. She was so used to walking on eggshells, she'd spent a lifetime doing that and had unknowingly applied her mother's reactions to things to the entire world.

She almost laughed. "Yeah. Sorry about that, too."

He turned his focus back to the road. "So, what's the Christmas tree story you started back there when you were trying to distract Sam from my unemployment details?"

"Oh, nothing," she said, now not wanting to have to get into her childhood stories.

"We've got a long, slow drive back thanks to this weather. Also, I think you owe my injured pride a story," he said, an adorable half smile gracing his face.

She groaned. "It really isn't much of a story at all. My mom just promised to let me pick a tree one year and then didn't."

He frowned. "There are so many holes in that story I don't even know where to begin. Why don't you tell me the real story with all the details you're trying to keep out of it?"

She leaned her head back. "Fine. I had researched Montana tree farms for a project in school and received an A+. So my mother said that I could pick whatever tree I wanted. I wanted the Balsam fir. Then Molly brought home an A+ on a science exam, and she let her pick the tree. It wasn't Molly's fault. She didn't even know what my mother had agreed to. See? Boring story. Nothing big."

He didn't say anything for what felt like minutes. "Kind of setting the stage for sibling rivalry?"

She didn't want to admit she'd fallen for it and that she was horribly jealous of her sister. She had been the petty one in their entire relationship. "Yeah. I guess."

"Was there a lot of that kind of thing?"

You have no idea.

She stared at the dark road, watching the way the headlights hit the snow blowing. Telling Finn about the way things used to be—the way *she* used to be—was embarrassing. Worse than embarrassing. The way she'd felt about her sisters filled her with shame. She had been so much like her mother, and *no one* liked her mother. He would never understand because he had come from the perfect family and his brother was his best friend. There were so many memories that she barely let herself think about because the moment she did, heat would flood her body and she'd feel like running away... from all of them.

Moving back to Shadow Creek had been the best thing for her relationship with her sisters. Secrets had been revealed, and old wounds had been healed. But it also meant facing her past and her mistakes daily. When she didn't live near family, it was easy to just focus on her patients, on her career, and compartmentalize. She hadn't counted on the daily feelings of regret she had. She didn't want to be that insecure and petty girl she used to be, but she was forced to remember her every day in Shadow Creek.

She glanced over at Finn, knowing she owed him some kind of reply. "There was. I mean, it wasn't healthy. I'm not like that anymore," she said, cringing because her voice sounded desperate, like she was trying to defend herself when he hadn't accused her of anything.

"Of course not. Everyone has stuff in their past they aren't proud of. I guess the goal is to recognize that and actually do something about it. There are people who go through life repeating the same mistakes over and over again and never even *try* to change. You and your sisters look pretty close now."

She let his words sink in for several long moments. He had assumed the best in her. Finn saw her as more and believed that she had changed; he'd taken her word for it. Even though he knew firsthand just how far she had been willing to go to compete with Molly. Far enough to ask him to the prom.

She quickly tossed that thought aside because it was too embarrassing. "We're close because Molly is forgiving," she blurted out before she could stop herself. Or maybe she wanted to tell him. Maybe a part of her wanted his honest opinion. Then this…whatever it was she was feeling between them would be over, because he would see her for the person she really was.

He pulled into the snow-filled driveway and parked before turning to her. "Why do you always do that? You never give yourself credit for anything."

She swallowed hard, her heart racing in her chest, pounding, as she stared into his blue eyes. The words she'd held onto for so long refused to come out.

Finn reached out and placed his hand over hers, and tears stung her eyes, because the gesture reminded her of when she'd done the same to him. She couldn't back down now.

"It's okay, Mel," he said, in a voice that was tender and gruff and made her feel the safest she'd ever felt in her life.

"I'm the reason Molly and Ben broke up and the reason she stayed away from Shadow Creek for so long," she choked out. "I'm the reason she left Shadow Creek for so many years. If I hadn't been such a jealous brat, she would have been able to confide in me. She had no one at home."

He frowned. "What are you talking about?"

The sound of Molly's voice, telling her she needed space and to concentrate on school, played over her mind as it had so many nights. She should have known Molly would never shut them out without a reason. She should have listened harder, beneath the words, to the pain her sister was hiding.

She nodded rapidly, trying to pull her hand from his, but he held on. "If I hadn't been so jealous of her all the time, she would have called me. Addie was too young, but Molly would have called me if I hadn't been so nasty to her. She would have confided in me, and I would have rushed over to her dorm room, and I would have hugged her and told her none of it was her fault. I would have called the police. And I would have called Ben. He would have helped her. She wouldn't have had to deliver that baby girl without any of us knowing. I would have been there for her. I could have helped her. But instead, I believed everything our mom told us—that Molly was concentrating on school and her career and didn't have time for distractions. I believed all of it. And a part of me was happy that I was finally the apple of my mother's eye," she said, squeezing her eyes shut, so angry with herself, *refusing* to shed a tear for the terrible sister she'd been.

Finn swore softly and then leaned across and pulled her into him. She buried her face in the crook of his neck, drinking in his fresh scent, his strength. "You couldn't have known. Ben didn't find out until Molly came home and told him. You were played by your mom."

She shook her head against him. "But I should have—"

"*No*. It's not your fault, Mel. It's not. You have to let this go. No one blames you for any of it. You have to stop."

His words impacted more than she thought they ever would be able to. But she heard the tenderness, the sincerity in his deep voice. She felt his strength and support as he held her close to him. And the strange feeling of relief swept over her. She had told someone. Finn. And he hadn't questioned her. He'd believed her. He'd sounded angry…for her. He told her it wasn't her fault.

His lips brushed against her head, and a shiver ran through her. She pulled back, awkwardly, raising her eyes to his. What she saw there made her breath catch. He was staring at her like no man had. Like no one had ever stared at her before. He was staring at her like he *knew* her. Knew who she was, deep inside.

And that terrified her.

"We should go inside, before all the food goes bad." She hopped out of the truck, the cold blast of wind and snow hitting her overheated face. Something was happening to her. Something that felt amazing and yet was nothing she could allow herself to feel.

It felt a lot like falling for her fake boyfriend.

Chapter Seven

"How about I cook dinner and you decorate the tree?" Finn suggested, putting the last of the groceries in the fridge. The tree was already positioned in the stand and was tucked nicely in the corner where the fireplace wall was. He had to admit it already looked good without an ornament on it. It filled up the space and was tall, but the peaked ceilings accommodated it perfectly.

Melody was the other thing who fit perfectly in here. He had come to this cabin to get away from everyone and their expectations and their opinions. He hadn't missed company—even though he enjoyed and appreciated Ben and Molly and his mother's visits, he'd been content in solitude. When Melody had first shown up, he'd immediately felt trapped, and at first, he'd been on guard, careful to not let any of his true feelings out. But in just a few short days, he found himself looking forward to seeing her in the morning. In fact, he went to bed at night with an anticipation of their breakfast chat or arguing over exercise equipment. Their day in town together had been the best he'd had in a long time.

He felt like he was finally getting to know the real her...and he liked what he saw.

Melody projected that she had it all together, but when she had finally opened up a little, she damn well near broke his heart. He knew a lot of what had happened to Molly but from Ben's perspective. He would never have assumed that Melody blamed herself for not being there for her sister and that she could have eased her pain enough to change the course of events that unfolded.

The more Melody revealed about herself, the more he felt connected to her and the more he found himself drawn to her. She was hard on herself, and he identified with that, even if it was painful to witness.

More than anything, he wanted to be able to help her forgive herself and move on. What had happened in Molly's life had been brutally unfair and tragic. Melody taking any part of that blame wouldn't get her anywhere. Ben still blamed himself for letting Molly walk away from him so many years ago and not pushing for answers at the time. He knew all of them were coming from a place of love because they all hated what had happened to Molly.

"What are you cooking?" she asked, pulling him from his thoughts. She was currently standing in front of the tree with the box of ornaments.

"How about a stir-fry?" He pulled out some vegetables.

She turned around slowly. "Like, with real vegetables, not in their powdered form?"

He straightened his shoulders. "Obviously."

She raised an eyebrow. "Is it?"

He tried not to smile as he pulled out the broccoli—broccoli had never made him smile, but Melody did. He washed and chopped vegetables while she added ornaments to the tree. "Should we put Christmas music on or something?" It was too quiet, and he found himself wanting to know more, to fill the silence with questions, but he didn't want to push.

She nodded. "Probably a good idea. And, bonus, we'll have something lined up for when everyone gets here tomorrow."

"Agreed." He flipped through the pre-set stations until Mariah Carey's voice filled the open space with her declaration of what she wanted for Christmas. He rolled his shoulders and glanced out the window. The snow hadn't let up at all. In fact, it looked as though there was more snow than sky, and the wind rattled the windows every now and then.

"I'm going to grab a sweater," Melody said, folding her arms across her chest as she stepped back from the tree.

"Are you cold? I could light a fire." He wiped his hands all over Santa's cheerful face on the dishtowel and tossed it onto the counter.

Melody's face lit up, and she gave him a smile that almost had him tripping over his feet. "That would be great!"

Warmth flushed his chest. That odd feeling of contentment, of his life feeling right, flittered through him. Because of her joy. He made his way over to the stack of logs by the fireplace, making a mental note to get some more from the porch later, and lit the fire, humming along to the Christmas music. He gripped the edge of the fireplace ledge to stand, grimacing slightly as he stood. But even his leg didn't feel as bad. "There, that'll warm up the place pretty quick," he said.

Melody glanced over at him and smiled. "Thanks."

"Tree is looking good," he said, joining her.

She handed him a few snowman ornaments. "Want to hang those near the top?"

"Sure," he said, taking them from her. That spark that he felt every time his body made contact with hers ran through him, and he was very aware of how close they were standing.

He remembered how soft her hair had felt against his lips, how perfect she had felt in his arms.

Then immediately kicked himself because those moments weren't about attraction, but comfort.

"Dinner is smelling good," she said, turning to him. With the direction his thoughts were going, he wished she hadn't. Up close, it was hard not to notice just how gorgeous she was. Her eyes sparkled and her full lips were rosy, and she reminded him of how good life could be. Like somewhere along the way he'd forgotten that. He'd been so focused on his injury and everything that had been taken away from him instead on the fact that he was here. He was alive.

He smiled at her, backing up a step. "Thanks. I better get back to it," he said, needing to distance himself from her. Half an hour later, he was plating their chicken stir-fry and rice and Melody was peering into the fridge to get drinks.

"I guess its beer or...orange juice or eggnog? Though I guess that's for family."

"Definitely beer. I think they said they'll bring all that stuff. Where do you want to sit?"

She grabbed two bottles of beer and glanced at the table and then the couches. "How about we sit on the couch and watch a movie or something?"

"No sappy Christmas movies," he said, settling into the corner of one couch while Melody sat in the corner of the other, a side table between them. Perfect. Less temptation.

"Agreed."

He shrugged and put his feet on the coffee table ottoman. "Too happy."

She nodded, taking a forkful of food. "True, but we're supposed to be happy."

"How about *Die Hard*?"

"Perfect! Also, this food is delicious."

He'd just started the movie when both their phones

vibrated. They looked at each other. "It's borderline harassment," he said. "I thought they were all busy professionals."

She rolled her eyes. "I know."

"Do you want to look or should I?"

She flashed him a smile that would have made him agree to just about anything. "You can do the honors as my doting boyfriend."

My God, he might just turn into one of those doting boyfriends if she kept looking at him like that. He picked up his phone, reading the text aloud. "*'Hey guys, sorry to say that we won't be able to come up tomorrow because the roads are closed because of the storm. We'll be there Christmas Eve morning, though. Stay warm!'*"

Melody frowned and looked in the direction of the windows. "It can't be *that* bad. We still have power," she said.

He was already looking up the weather. "It's bad. Worse than bad. White-out conditions, possible power outages due to high winds."

"Oh, great. One day later is perfect. We won't have to fake joy for as long," she said, finishing off the food on her plate.

He nodded, though both of them had seemed a lot less miserable the last couple days. Especially after their trip into town. Unless she'd been faking it? *He* wasn't.

He frowned and worked on his own plate. Melody settled back in the sofa and picked up her beer, her eyes on the television. A part of him was very happy to not have to give up his time with her. The lights and television flickered momentarily, and they both let out a sigh of relief when they stayed on.

"I guess there isn't a generator?" Melody said, glancing over at him.

He shook his head. "No. But there's enough wood for a

few days if the power did go out."

"But then we wouldn't be able to watch the rest of the *Die Hard* movies," she complained, but her eyes sparkled.

He sighed. "There you go speaking the worst into existence again."

She laughed, and just like that, the lights flickered and all power went out. The fireplace glowed, and Melody turned to him. "Oops."

"We've really got to work on your powers of suggestion. Focus them on good, not evil."

She grinned, and his chest warmed at the amusement plain on her face. No. She wasn't faking it, either.

It was one thing to be around Melody and have lots of activities planned. It was another to sit in a dark cabin all night, warmth and laughter still hovering between them. The room had gone from friendly and bright to firelight flickering and intimate. It was so silent except for the whirring of wind outside. "Now what are we going to do?"

He got up and walked to the window, intending to assess however much of the situation he could despite the dark. They probably weren't going to get power for hours if this storm didn't let up. "Good thing we stocked up on beer."

She joined him at the window. Immediately, he wished she hadn't, because they were standing very close to each other.

"Are you implying that beer would be necessary when stuck with me in a storm?" she asked softly.

His mouth went dry, and he looked down into her sparkling eyes. "Don't put words into my mouth," he said with a short laugh, moving away from her and into safer territory. The kitchen was safe. Dirty dishes were definitely safe.

"How about a board game?" She crossed the great room and opened the armoire that housed extra blankets and pillows…and apparently board games.

He got busy loading the dishwasher and tried to pull himself together. "Sure."

"Monopoly?"

"Sounds good."

"I should warn you. I can get pretty competitive," she said, opening the box and setting it up on the ottoman coffee table.

He bit back a smile and headed for the fridge. More beer was definitely in order. "Perfect. Me too. Once, Ben and I were so obsessed with it as kids, our mom had to hide the game. We kept playing best of three series, and when Saturday night hit, we stayed up all night. Big trouble once we were discovered."

She started counting out the bills. "Who was the ultimate champ?"

"A tie. We still haven't had our tie-breaker game," he said, sitting down opposite her.

Two hours and two more beers later, Finn came to the conclusion that Melody was actually more competitive than him and Ben combined. She was counting her piles of cash, and he knew she was checking if she had enough money to buy hotels on Boardwalk and Park Place, her eyes glittering with impending victory. Little did she know he wasn't the type to go down that easily. He stretched his bad leg out in front of him and groaned, clutching his thigh.

She put down her wad of cash and leaned forward, the evil gleam gone, replaced by a frown of concern. "Are you okay?"

He winced and took a deep breath. "Yeah. Yeah, I'm fine. It's your turn," he said, finishing off his beer, his hand still on his leg.

She bit her lower lip, her gaze going from him to her pile of cash. He stifled his grin when she made the move he thought she would and just rolled the dice, intentionally missing her opportunity to buy property. "Your turn. I hate the Chance pile," she said under her breath after having to fork over cash for a card she picked up from the Chance deck.

He cleared his throat and proceeded to place hotels on all the green, yellow, and red properties he owned. He shifted uncomfortably when she swore under her breath, and her eyes narrowed on him. "Did you set me up? Did you fake leg pain so that I would *feel sorry for you and not buy hotels*?"

He straightened some errant hotels, not looking at her. "Maybe."

"This means war, Finn," she said, leaning forward.

He sat back, enjoying the taste of impending victory. "I welcome the challenge."

She made a strangled noise and picked up her beer. "This is empty," she said, putting down the bottle with an audible *thud*.

"I'll get you another one."

"Oh, is your *leg* all right? Are you sure you can manage standing?"

He bit back a grin and stood then held back a curse when he put his weight on his injured leg. Dammit. Sitting on the rug for so long in the same position, due to their competitive nature, had him regretting all of it.

"Nice try," she grumbled, making piles with her five-hundred-dollar bills. "No more sympathy from me. I'll be sitting here counting all my money and then mentally calculating how many times it will take for you to land on my property before you go bankrupt."

He was relieved. He didn't want her sympathy now that he actually *was* in pain. He walked slowly so that his limp wouldn't be too pronounced and then leaned against the island to take a break, his heart racing. Damn. It felt like he'd just run a mile. He'd had too much to drink to make him think of touching pain meds, but not taking anything would be hell, too. His only option was another beer and then coming up with an excuse to end the game and going to his own room where he could either try and sleep it off or stare at the ceiling in misery.

"I think we need more wood," Melody called out.

Shit. Normally, grabbing a few logs from the porch would be nothing he'd think twice about. Now it would be sheer torture. Especially without letting Melody know. He hobbled over to the door. "I'll grab it. Just sit there and try and come up with a game plan to win. But there's no way you're getting through that alley of death I just set up."

"Nice try. I actually have enough money to put hotels on St. Charles and that entire row, which comes *before* your overpriced property, so we'll see who needs a game plan."

He opened the front door, and wind and snow hit him in the face as he limped onto the porch. He shut the door behind him, almost relieved by the cold on his overheated skin. He slowly made his way to the pile of wood and grabbed a few logs. But because it was so dark out, he picked the wrong one, and it sent a few others piling out. He reached out to try and grab them before it sent the whole pile tumbling, inadvertently putting his weight on his bad leg, and it gave out. He reached out for something to steady himself but ended up causing the entire pile to collapse around him. He swore, and tears stung his eyes as he landed on his ass on the porch. He squeezed his eyes shut against the throbbing, searing pain in his leg and the sudden nausea that gripped him.

He heard the door opening and Melody rushing over to him. "Omigosh, Finn. Are you okay? Why didn't you let me help you?"

Humiliation burned through his body. "I can get a damn piece of wood," he snapped and then instantly regretted his harsh tone.

"This isn't the time for macho bravado," she said in an

equally snippy voice. "Clearly you need help because you're sitting on your ass in a blizzard. So let me help you up."

He clenched his teeth and opened his eyes. "I can get up myself."

She sat back on her heels and crossed her arms, raising a brow. "Then go."

Dammit. He glanced over at the pile of wood, or what had been a pile of wood, and knew it would be ugly. "Fine. For the record, you're not a very nice girlfriend. I just need you to help me stand. Once I'm standing, I can walk. It was just a small mess-up and all the logs came tumbling down. I'm actually fine."

"Sure you are. Just like you were going to actually win that game of Monopoly. Also, I *am* a very nice girlfriend, and if you can't appreciate me, then that's your own fault." She stood and held out her hand, not an ounce of sympathy in her voice. Clearly, she knew him better than he thought.

He almost managed a laugh, but the pain in his leg was so severe he only managed a grunt as he surrendered his pride and reached for Melody's hand. Her grip was firm and she was strong, tucking one of her shoulders under his left arm and wrapping her arm around his waist once he was standing. "Just lean on me as much as you want. I'm a lot tougher than you think."

He gritted his teeth hard, concentrating on just making it inside to the couch and hopefully not falling on top of her. He had thought a hoist up would do the trick, but he really did need the help. And he was pissed. None of this should have happened.

"We're almost there. You're doing great," she said, the encouragement in her voice making him cringe. He liked it better when she was angry at him. He hated that she was seeing him like this. He hated *being* like this. When they reached the couch, he hesitated, knowing he was in for a hell of a time trying to go from standing to lying down. He just needed to lie down and that would be okay.

"I'm okay," he said through gritted teeth, moving his arm away, wishing she could just go away and give him some privacy. "You can go back to counting your money."

She blinked. "I'm not just going to leave you standing here. How are you going to actually get on the couch without being in intense misery? Here's what we're going to do: you're going to put both hands on my shoulders. I'll hold onto your waist and slowly crouch down."

"Why are you so bossy?" he grumbled.

"Because you're too proud to accept my help and just listen to me."

"I'm going to drag you down on top of me," he said, not taking any pleasure in the idea of Melody on top of him in this condition.

"You are forgetting I work in a hospital and have had many heavily pregnant and distraught women in vulnerable positions. Believe me, I can handle you. I've never dropped someone. Let's go. Trust me. I've got you," she said firmly.

He shut his eyes. He had no choice. Gritting his teeth, he did as he was told, but trying to lean on her as little as possible. He let out a litany of curses as he finally hit the couch, blinding pain making him see stars instead of Melody's gorgeous face. But she was right there, crouched beside him, a deep frown on her forehead. "What can I do to help? What kind of pain is it?"

He squeezed his eyes shut. "It's like a muscle spasm. It was damaged in the fire, and it tightens uncontrollably. It will loosen up," he said, opening his eyes and staring at the ceiling, hoping like hell it would hurry up.

"What about a heating pad?"

He gave a shake of his head. "No heat."

"Can I massage it? Loosen the tension?"

How the hell would Melody's hands on his thigh loosen any kind of tension? He moved his hand to his thigh. "It's okay. It's already easing up," he lied, trying to apply pressure himself.

She swatted his hand away. "You're a bad liar. Just like you're a bad Monopoly player. Show me where and what you like."

Oh, for God's sake. She needed to stop talking. Her hands gently grasped the sides of his thigh, and he clenched his teeth from the pain. Thankfully, all sexual thoughts left his head due to his physical agony. "Right there," he managed.

She slowly, gently, kneaded his leg, and he forced himself to relax. She applied gentle but firm pressure, and slowly, thankfully, after a few minutes he felt the knot in his leg beginning to uncoil.

"I can feel your muscle loosening," she said softly.

"You can stop if you're tired," he said, speaking with greater ease now. He could actually take a deep breath now that the pain was lessening.

"I'll go a bit longer until I don't feel the knot anymore."

"Thank you," he said, completely humbled and grateful.

"No problem. It reminds me of the time I helped Addie make homemade pizza dough."

"My leg is not like pizza dough," he said in a choked voice. "It has way more muscle than that."

She burst out laughing. "Your ego is too easy to bait."

He grimaced. "I can't deny it."

"I feel bad. If I hadn't been winning at Monopoly and beating you so badly, you wouldn't have had to drink so much, and you would've been able to take some painkillers."

He laughed. Actually laughed. And maybe fell for her just a little bit more as she crouched on the floor beside him. She didn't feel sorry for him. She didn't put up with his stubbornness. She was tough and knew exactly how to deal with him. He didn't think he'd ever forget what she'd done for him here.

He wanted to reach out and move the strands of hair that kept falling in front of her eyes as she worked on his leg, but he knew that would be crossing a line. It would be too intimate. Because then he'd want more. He'd want to touch the side of her face, to trace her cheekbone, then lower, until he reached her mouth. He wanted to feel if her lips were as soft as they looked.

Without thinking of the repercussions of a simple touch, he placed his hand on hers, and she stopped moving. He'd meant to just stop her from continuing to work on his leg, because he knew she would have kept going. But instead, it ignited a spark in him that he didn't want to ignore anymore.

Her mouth parted, and she looked at him with the same desire sparkling in her eyes that he felt. "Better?" she whispered.

He gave her a stiff nod. "Thank you."

She slipped her hand from his and stood. "Well, do you want to turn in for the night?"

Sitting up, he managed to swing his leg over the side of the sofa. "Nope. I've got a second wind. You're a miracle worker. My leg feels so much better. Thanks, Mel."

She shrugged and sat on the couch opposite him. "No big deal, really. I mean, what else were we going to do with our time?"

His eyes went to her mouth then back up to her eyes when he realized what he was doing. Her face had turned red, and he needed to stop. This was just two people stranded alone together for the holidays. Two lonely people who, once they left this perfect little cabin of happiness, would re-enter the real world and know they were wrong for each other. They had different long-term goals. Family was everything to him. One day, he wanted a family of his own, so starting something with someone who clearly didn't want those same things would be pointless. Besides, he needed to figure out what he was going to do with his career—though tonight was a grim predictor of what he *wasn't* going to be able to do. If the random spasms didn't completely go away, he would be a liability as a firefighter. He'd endanger the lives of people he was supposed to rescue, as well as his own crew. He had no idea where that would leave him. Even if he passed the physical, a random episode like tonight could make the difference between life and death.

"Want to continue our game?" he asked, tearing his gaze from hers.

Her face lit up. "Uh, yeah, because I think I was about to witness your demise."

He stood slowly, carefully allowing his leg to adjust to his full weight. "Okay, let's move it to the kitchen table if you don't mind," he said, picking up the board.

She started gathering the cash. "Not at all, but careful you don't lose our spots."

He let the pieces slide on purpose.

She let out a shriek that had him laughing like a kid. "Finn!"

"Don't worry. I have a photographic memory. Do you remember who had what hotels where?"

She made a strangled noise. "You're *not* going to win by cheating. Look where that got you last time—on your butt in the snow, surrounded by firewood."

He crossed the room, not even bothering to hide his limp. There was basically no point in hiding anymore. "What are you talking about? I'm just a poor firefighter who was injured when I crashed through a floor as I tried to rescue a child. Now, I'm just a shell of the man I used to be and have to hide in a remote cabin in the woods with a beard to mask my sadness."

There was silence for a second, and then Melody burst out laughing. "That's *shameless*. You're the same man. The same man you were. Just...grumpier. And possibly more diabolical."

He flashed her a smile. "Thanks."

Melody marched right by him and started setting up the pieces at the table. "Nice try. I can identify manipulation when I see it. You're forgetting who raised me."

That was funny. But it also wasn't. In fact, if she was ever comfortable enough to tell him, he wanted to know more about what she'd been through. Maybe talking to him about it would help like talking to her had helped him. There was a painful insecurity that she tried to keep hidden, and it bothered him to realize that she was so hard on herself.

He also knew that she was probably still embarrassed about their own brief history. He wanted to right that. He didn't want her misinterpreting his rejection even though it was so many years ago. "Hey, do you remember the time you asked me to go to prom and I said no?"

He cringed at how that came out. It was probably so out of left field, and he should have broached it with a little more delicacy. Her face turned bright red, and then she covered it with her hands. "If this is a strategy to throw me off my Monopoly game, that is very shrewd and cold, Finn. Not at all what I'd expect from you."

"Sorry," he murmured, filling the gap between them. He gently pried her hands from her face. She stared up at him, her face bright red, but her eyes were filled with gut-wrenching humiliation. He regretted every inaccurate assumption he'd ever had about her. He held her hands in his, and for a second, he thought she was going to pull away from him and just leave.

"No, you don't have to be sorry. I do. I'm sorry I asked you to go to prom with me. You were right—it wasn't just because I wanted to go with you. I mean, I would have loved to go with you—I thought you were amazing—but I had no time for guys or friends. My entire life was focused on getting my mother's approval and being better than Molly. I was even jealous of Molly and Ben's relationship. *That's* why I asked you to prom. Because if Molly had Ben, then I wanted you."

Tears filled her eyes, but she blinked rapidly and took a labored breath. "If I had known everything that was going to happen after, then I would have been a better person. I would have been a better sister to Molly, and then maybe she wouldn't have had to go through what she did alone. Maybe I could have spared her everything," she said, and this time, the tears actually spilled from her eyes.

When she made a move to run from him, he pulled her into his arms. She was as stiff as a board for a moment, and then she wrapped her arms around him and cried. It was the only time he'd ever seen her cry or be emotional, and he held onto her tighter because her pain affected him. Her self-loathing was painful to witness. She had been going around carrying all this guilt and blaming herself for what her sister had endured.

"Hey," he said, unable to stop himself from letting his lips graze over the top of her head. "You are way too hard on yourself. Everything that happened in your life led you to the person you are now. You thought I was amazing? Well, I think *you're* amazing, Melody. Your sisters love you. You are not the girl your mother forced you to be, and it's not your fault that you were ever that way. You were set up to fail, and you have to let go of that guilt. It's not who you are now. It's hard to change. And you did and you need to give yourself some credit for that."

He pulled back slightly to look at her. His first mistake was raising his hands to cup the sides of her face, telling himself that he was only trying to be a friend, to be there for her. "The prom thing is water under the bridge. I said no to you because I didn't think you weren't interested in me, and I knew it was some kind of a plan that had nothing to do with us."

His second mistake was grazing his thumb over her cheekbone and pulling her closer instead of stepping back.

"Thank you for being so kind to me," she whispered.

He frowned. "I'm not being kind. That's actually what I think. You don't see yourself the way the rest of the world does. The way I do."

Her mouth dropped open. "Finn…"

He clenched his teeth, his gaze going from her eyes to her mouth. He couldn't remember a time in his life he'd wanted to kiss a woman as much as this. A time where he'd wanted to just stay in one moment because it felt so right. But he couldn't walk away from her without telling her the rest, without her believing him. "If you asked me now to prom, I'd say yes. If you asked me for anything right now, I'd say yes."

"Finn," she whispered again, his name sounding more like a plea, making him forget all the reasons this was a bad idea.

His third mistake was slipping his fingers into the silky hair at her nape and slowly lowering his head, his lips brushing against hers. "Mel," he said, half hoping she'd pull away and all their problems would be solved.

But she didn't. She reached up and wrapped her arms around his neck, and he tasted and reveled in a moment he'd never expected. But Melody was so much more than he ever expected. He deepened the kiss, and she pressed her soft curves against his body, like she trusted herself with him. He left one hand in her hair and let the other roam over the side of her body, wanting more. She'd reached a part of him he'd thought was gone, lost in the fire along with so much of him. She pulled at his heartstrings and drew him out of himself.

He stopped thinking about himself and his problems when he was around her. He was able to enjoy the moment. With her.

She ran her hands down his chest and up his arms, and he knew that neither of them planned this and neither of them could really take this further because it shouldn't go further. The last thing he wanted to do was hurt her.

He slowly, and with excruciating self-discipline, leaned back slightly. But her eyes were filled with desire and her cheeks flushed, and it made him forget about self-control and their family. He leaned down and kissed that soft spot beneath her ear. She made a soft sound that ignited a fire in him that he was going to have to ignore. Because even though she'd pretended her entire life that she was so tough, he knew that deep down she hid an insecurity that was dangerous. They had different goals, different dreams, and these feelings weren't real. They were here because they were forced in this cabin together. Just the thought of her helping him off his ass robbed every ounce of desire he had.

He pulled away, trying to not act like a jerk, like he was rejecting her. "We should probably stop."

She blinked, her eyes focusing, her pink cheeks turning an even deeper shade. "Right. Of course. Um…because we're a fake couple. We have to do better at remembering that." She backed away from him and turned to the board.

"Right."

He shoved his hands into his pockets, his own thoughts and insecurities railroading through him. He wasn't the same man. If one thing had led to another, they would have made it to the couch. How would he have even gotten on the couch? And then what? Everything he was once capable was now… unknown. He ran a hand over his jaw. The thought of not being a real couple didn't sound as funny as it did a week ago.

"I think I'll just clean up the game and stuff. Maybe

another beer, too," she said, the awkwardness in her voice almost making him cringe. He hated himself because he'd just finished apologizing for prom and telling her that if she asked for anything he'd say yes. He was an ass, and he should never had said that. It implied…things. Things that couldn't happen. He wanted to know more. He wanted to know about that haunted look in her eyes, why she had left the hospital. And he wanted to know who she *did* end up going to prom with. But none of this was his business.

He opened his mouth to tell her that he was sorry. For all of this. But there was nothing he could say that would make any of this better. "Good night."

She held his gaze, chin high, her green eyes glittering with pride.

He didn't want to walk away, but he did.

Chapter Eight

Melody watched Finn walk away, feeling like she'd just had everything she'd ever wanted taken away from her. Tonight, laughing with him...and then kissing him...yes, he was everything she didn't know she wanted.

She had never had a better night in her entire life. She had never felt so comfortable with someone else. She felt like he accepted her just as she was. And she *liked* who she was when she was with him. She liked *him*. She liked kissing him. No, she *loved* kissing him. Kissing Finn had been even better than she'd ever fantasized. It was one of those experiences she'd read about—weak knees, racing heart, and complete loss of control.

Except he'd had control. He'd been able to end things between them. Even though he'd said in that deep, mouth-wateringly raspy voice, *If you asked me now to prom, I'd say yes. If you asked me for anything right now, I'd say yes.*

That should have been the beginning of a beautiful relationship. Except it was the end of something that could never start. It was the end of something that had always been one-sided. He'd been this cute, popular, happy-go-lucky guy who would never be interested in her. She wouldn't even know what to do with all that happiness anyway. Maybe that's why now he'd spared her a second glance—because life had thrown him a nasty curveball. It didn't matter. None of what happened in this Hallmark cottage in the woods mattered. She was leaving Shadow Creek. She couldn't go back to that hospital or her mother.

She stood in the empty room, the fire just a small flicker of light. The draft from the storm blew through the room—or maybe it was in her head. Maybe it just felt cold because Finn was gone.

She never should have confided in him about Molly. She had exposed too much. Everything. At least that was how it felt. She wrapped her arms around herself, shivering as she grabbed a blanket off the couch.

Finn walked back into the room, and she held her breath. The room was lit just enough that she could make out his features. Finn was all good angles, all the time. "I forgot about the fire. I'll throw on a couple of more logs. Doesn't look like the storm will let up anytime soon. I guess you could sleep on the couch in here. I'll check throughout the night to make sure there's enough wood on the fire."

She huddled further into the red, Sherpa-lined blanket. "You don't have to do that, but thanks."

He nodded once. "I'll grab a flashlight and go to bed," he said, not sounding anything like the Finn who'd kissed her. Now he was back to sounding like the Finn when she'd first arrived at the cabin.

"Aren't you going to be cold?" she blurted before he could leave.

He stopped, holding a flashlight he'd taken from the cupboard atop the fridge. "Nope. I'll be fine."

"Oh."

He let out a rough sigh and shoved one hand in his pocket. "Mel?"

"Yes?" She tried to sound nonchalant, even though she could feel his mood had shifted.

"Who did you go to prom with?"

Her stomach dropped and rolled as a wave of nausea hit. It was one thing to have been shut down by him and an entirely other thing to admit the entire humiliation surrounding her prom. "Oh, um, you know…I didn't bother going. Who actually goes to their own prom anyway?" she asked, tempted to lift the blanket over her head and hide like a child. But because she couldn't do that, she sat still, at one with the nausea and humiliation as he slowly walked toward her.

"Why didn't you go?" His voice was raspy, his face drawn. She kind of hoped he'd sit on the couch opposite her, because she was pretty sure her humiliation was palpable. But no, Finn sat right beside her, his elbow on the back of the couch, leaning toward her like they were…something.

She averted her gaze. "Is there any brandy left? I think the beer has worn off."

He reached out and grasped her hand. "Hey, it's me, your boyfriend. You can tell me."

She stared at his larger hand on hers, relished its warmth and strength. When was the last time someone reached out to comfort her? She didn't know what to do with that. She didn't know how to lean into what he was offering, to let herself be completely honest. And the, "*Hey, it's me,*" meant something. Like Finn was an "it's me," and she'd had so few of those in her lifetime.

She tried to shake off the embarrassment. He had to know enough about her mother through Ben to not be too surprised at this. "No one else asked me and, um, going by myself would have been too humiliating. I didn't really have a lot of time for friends in high school. Or guys. Or, you know, basically anything half normal," she said with a sharp laugh that sounded high-pitched and awkward to her ears.

The sympathy that flooded his eyes comforted her. That was a first. There was no judgment as he looked at her. There was just that delicious warmth that made her want to believe that they could be something together, that made her feel like it was okay to be vulnerable, that he was safe.

He reached out and framed one side of her face with his hand. "I'm sorry. I'm sorry I didn't say yes." He leaned forward and kissed her.

It was over a heartbeat later when he pulled back.

Disappointment shot through her, and she held his gaze, deciding she didn't want to end this. She didn't want him to leave and go to bed. And she didn't want to stop talking to him. For the first time, maybe since she'd learned that she always had to be perfect, she wanted to confide in someone. Finn. Because she knew he wouldn't judge her. "I don't want to go back," she said softly.

His brows pulled together. "Shadow Creek?"

She nodded. "Or the hospital."

He put his hand on her thigh, the warmth seeping through her, the gesture intimate and sincere. "What happened?"

She turned away. She had thought she'd be able to just say it, to just blurt it out because he was so easy to talk to. But the reality, the vividness of the memory, rose to the surface with an intensity she wasn't prepared for. "I screwed up so badly, Finn," she said, her voice breaking.

"No, you didn't," he said, squeezing her thigh gently, leaning forward so that she was forced to make eye contact with him. He had this faith in her that was so immediate and so genuine and so addictive that she didn't want to keep speaking. She wanted to sit in this spot where she felt wholly and completely accepted. She wanted to cling to the feeling of someone believing in her. But she had to tell him the rest of it. She had to talk about it.

She pulled the words from deep down inside. "I should have known. If I could go back...maybe I could have been faster. I could have gotten that baby out sooner," she said, squeezing her eyes shut, but then was just tormented by the image of the operating room. Of the baby. Of the parents. The sounds that shouldn't have been there, the sounds that should have but weren't. There was no baby's cry.

"What happened?" he asked, roughly, pulling her closer to him, and she willingly accepted everything he was offering, accepting someone else's strength for once.

"She was my patient; she'd just been in for her weekly check-up four days earlier, and everything was fine. She was thirty-eight weeks pregnant. Strong heartbeat. No complications. She was young and healthy...and then...then they came into the ER that night, and I was on-call. They were worried because she hadn't felt the baby move in more than twenty-four hours." She leaned her head against his shoulder, and he placed his arm on the nape of her neck and kissed the top of her head, not saying a word.

"We rushed her in for an ultrasound, and it wasn't good. There were very faint vitals, and I knew we needed to do an emergency C-section, and even then...I knew the chances were slim. I did everything, Finn. Everything. We all did. The entire team. We were so fast, so focused...but when I pulled that baby out..."

She wrapped her arms around his neck. She had been so alone for so long, so alone in her need to be perfect that she had forgotten just how much she needed people. Or maybe it had been Finn she'd needed all along. He pulled her onto his lap, and for the first time, she didn't care that she wasn't pulled together; she didn't care that she was crying in front of someone.

"That wasn't your fault, either," he said, his lips rasping

the top of her head as he spoke. "You know the statistics. You can't take on that kind of blame."

The relief in hearing him say that tugged at the rope she'd hung herself from the day that happened. There was a weightlessness that made her feel alive again, like when she was a little girl, on those rare occasions she'd sit on a swing and soar as high as she could, imagining what it would feel like to fly. She had been trapped for so long.

"I know. I know the numbers. I don't know why I thought I would be able to escape them, why I would be different. But that was the first baby I lost, and I can't shake it. I didn't know it would be this hard. I didn't know I could be this afraid of ever delivering a baby again. Oh my God, Finn. That poor couple," she said, holding onto him tightly, digging her hands into his strong arms.

He squeezed her closer. "You tried. You tried everything you could do. You're a good doctor. A *great* doctor. You know that."

"I can't do it again. I don't want to do it again," she said, not even trying to hide her tears as she pulled back to look at him. "I'm not who everyone thinks I am."

"Or you're so much *more* than you think you are. Maybe that's it," he said, his voice gruff, tender as he gently swept the tears from her face with his thumb.

"I'm so scared," she choked out.

"I get it. Hell, do I get it. But you have to push past that. What's your plan? Are you just going to throw years of hard work away? I know you're a talented doctor. You don't get to where you are at your age on luck."

She shook her head. "No, but I was having problems when I went back. I started getting anxiety attacks. That's never happened to me before. I never had issues with anxiety, and suddenly I was crawling out of my skin. I tried for a week, and then…I was told to take some time off. I've never taken time off."

"You're allowed to have a life, to hit a wall and need to walk away for a bit," he said.

She leaned forward and kissed him, because she wanted to be closer to him again, because he made her feel like herself, and she hadn't felt like herself in so long. Somewhere along the way, she'd lost track of who she was, of who she wanted to be. He kissed her back in that delicious way that she'd discovered only Finn could, threading his fingers in her hair. "You have to come back. You can't send me back there to deal with our family," he said, smiling against her neck as he trailed kisses against her skin.

"I wish we could just stay here forever and never go back to work."

Finn didn't think he'd ever experienced an attraction like this for anyone. Maybe because it was so much more than physical. He liked talking to her, hearing her thoughts, and he valued her opinion. But more than that, she was someone he could talk to—and he hadn't felt like he could really talk to anyone in a long time. "Me, too."

She snuggled further into him, and it felt like they had done this forever. "That night you told me about the accident, it felt like you stopped suddenly. Like there was more."

He was surprised that she remembered enough to ask him. No, he wasn't. Because he wanted to know everything about her, too. What felt impossible to say not that long ago felt completely normal now. "There wasn't much more. I don't talk about this to anyone, but the rest is what keeps me up at night and makes me think it's time for me to leave firefighting behind. We didn't have much time to think because for all we knew there could be a family in there. A kid. Kids. Babies.

You don't leave kids, you know? There was a huge volume of smoke, more than we expected, and we didn't realize it until it was too late, and by that point, we couldn't see a damn thing. But we heard a kid. We got this little guy out of the closet. And as I was following him and my partner, the floor just gave out from under me, and…that was the last thing I remember."

She turned in his arms and leaned up to kiss him. He held her head to his, knowing that in her own way she got him. When she pulled back, she ran her fingers over his jaw, the featherlight touch a contrast to the strength she had. "I'm glad you're here."

"Me, too. And since we're talking about not going back…I've been thinking a lot about what I would do if I didn't go back to being a firefighter." It felt strange to tell this to Melody when he hadn't told Ben yet, when he wasn't even sure himself. But he didn't want to keep anything from her. Melody had quickly become this person who he trusted, and he valued her opinion. Right here, in the dark, on this sofa, it's like his entire messed-up world finally made sense.

"Really?"

"Yeah. I know I've said that it's the only thing I would ever do with my life, but the closer I get to the New Year, the more I realize that I may never reach the level I need to be a firefighter again."

She ran a hand down his arm. "Finn, I'm sorry."

He swallowed past the lump in his throat. It was almost surreal to talk about this. A month ago, he wouldn't have been able to. Or maybe it was Melody, because a month ago he hadn't known her like this. "I need to start looking at it from a different angle. My dad didn't have a second chance. I do. So I can sit here and feel sorry for myself or I can start planning a future that is different from my original plan."

"I think that's a pretty hard conclusion to come to, but it's the right way to look at it. A plan B is always a good idea, especially one that you can get excited about. But are you sure that you're not giving up too soon? Healing sometimes doesn't fit into our ideal timeline, but it doesn't mean that it won't happen."

He shrugged. "You're right. That's why I don't want to make any rash decisions. I haven't decided yet, but I've been looking into a career as an arson investigator. Maybe work my way up to fire marshal someday."

"I think that's great."

"There is a lot I already know about it, and because I was a firefighter, the courses wouldn't even be that long. It's pretty specialized, and I don't think it would be difficult to get a job with my background," he said, stopping because suddenly all the doubts came crashing down around him. He could picture himself doing the job, he could see it as a reality, and maybe that's what was so terrifying. Life was throwing him in a different direction, and he didn't know if he actually wanted to go along with it.

"Finn?"

He ran a hand through his hair. "I don't know. Maybe this is all a mistake. Maybe I should just stay focused on getting my leg healed. There's that whole saying about 'never have a plan B' because then I'm not giving plan A my all. It feels messed up to be talking about another career. I've never had to think about it, you know?"

Her eyes clouded over. "I think anything that is so far away from where you thought your life would be will feel like that. It doesn't mean it's wrong. It just might take time to get used to the idea."

He nodded, rubbing the back of his neck. "Maybe that's it. I feel like I'm betraying Ben, too. I know what he'd say. He'd tell me to keep healing for as long as it takes. But I can't do that. I can't just sit around in their cabin in the middle of nowhere and not earn a living. There comes a point when it's time to change paths. I can't be afraid of that. I've never been afraid of anything."

"Then give yourself these last few weeks before the new year. Make some calls, do some research. You must have contacts in the industry. Reach out to them. Then make your decision so that on January first, you know exactly where you're going."

"I like the way you think," he said, feeling relieved to have this out there and Melody not think he was throwing his life away. He liked having a plan.

She gave him a gorgeous smile. "I'm glad. I'm learning to like the way I think, too."

He gave a short laugh. "What about you? Did you always want to be a doctor? Can you imagine yourself doing anything different?"

Her smile fell like a deck of cards. "Yes, I always wanted to be a doctor."

She was lying. But he had no idea why, and he was disappointed that she didn't want to share with him as well. "Really?"

She sighed, and her eyes darted guiltily away from his. "Okay, maybe not. I'm sorry. I don't know why I lied. It's weird. There are things…from my past, from my family, that are so messed up, and I've never talked to anyone about them. I've always lied and said I'm fine, that I'm doing exactly what I want to do, everything is perfect."

Any irritation vanished, and sympathy flooded him. He'd heard stories from Ben, not all and not in detail, but he knew Molly and Melody's mother, Marlene, was all a big show. "Well, considering we are stuck together for a while with no power, we might as well get to know each other. I've never broken a secret," he said, making an X over his heart.

She gave him a smile, a vulnerable one he hadn't seen from her before. She seemed younger and unsure of herself as she drew her knees up to her chest. "Sometimes I don't know if I ever really wanted to be a doctor. Lately, I've been thinking about my childhood. A lot. And I normally don't like to dwell on the past, but with the work stuff that's happened, I've been questioning everything. I wonder if I only wanted to be a doctor to please my mother, to compete with Molly."

That last sentence hung there, and he tried to hide his shock. She and Molly were so close he couldn't imagine her going so far as choosing a career to compete with her sister. He cleared his throat. "Would you really have gone through that many years of school, worked that hard, *just* to compete with Molly?"

She shrugged, her cheeks pink. "I don't know. I feel like I don't know anything about myself anymore. It's awful, isn't it?"

He pulled her closer, and she curled into him, like she needed him as much as he needed her. "You're not awful. But you *are* really hard on yourself."

She rested her face on his shoulder. "You don't know what I was like, Finn. Molly and I weren't like you and Ben. There was a time when I was so jealous of her, I could barely look at her. She was so smart. So pretty. So perfect. That snow globe at the general store? My mom bought one just like it for Molly one Christmas. Addie and I only got one gift each, and Molly had dozens. I had wanted that snow globe so badly, and I was so jealous that I purposely dropped it. The worst part is that Molly had planned on giving it to me when our mother wasn't around."

He kissed the top of her head, hating the self-hatred in her voice, but the snow globe at the store made more sense to him now. "You were a kid. You have to let it go, Mel."

"I know. I'm trying, but it's so intertwined in who I am. Our mother made a constant example of her. I was told over and over again that I would never be as smart as Molly. So all

I did was study. Hours. Well into the night. Molly skipped a grade without trying and got so many presents, and our mother lavished her with attention. Molly never even bragged about it—she was embarrassed and would always share with us.

"But that wasn't good enough for me. I was hell bent on skipping a grade, too, and did whatever it took. When I finally managed to get high enough grades, my mother told me that she knew I'd been putting in those long hours, that I wasn't naturally as gifted as Molly. She was right. I wasn't, and it killed me. When Molly said she wanted to be a doctor, our mom told everyone we would meet—at the grocery store, at school, at the doctor's office. I was desperate for that kind of attention. That's when I decided I was going to be a doctor, too."

"You honestly believe you survived medical school just to be like your sister? Even people who want to be doctors don't always survive."

She shrugged. "I have no idea what to think anymore, Finn. I don't know who I am."

"Do you love your job?"

She shrugged. "I did. Or I thought I did. Maybe I just liked the prestige, like my mom."

He held onto her tighter. "No. I don't buy that. You're not like your mom. You're not in it for the prestige. Don't do that to yourself. You're an incredible person, Mel. And I'm so glad that we got snowed in here together so I could find all that out."

He kissed her, feeling everything that had been missing from his life, right here in his arms. He didn't want to share their time with anyone. He didn't want to think about reality that would come barreling through that door in a day or two. And he didn't want to think about how their careers and lives were about to take them away from how happy they were right now.

Chapter Nine

Melody opened her eyes, startled by the fact that she felt… good. Safe. Happy. Warm. She blinked a few times and realized she was lying on the couch, half on top of Finn, who was still sleeping. It was still dark out, and the wind was still whistling. The fire had burned out, but she was nice and toasty next to him.

For the first time in as long as she could remember, she didn't check the time on her phone. She didn't hop out of bed. Instead, she put her head back down on Finn's chest, holding onto him, holding onto the feeling that everything was right or *could* be right. Nothing had been right in her world in so long…or maybe forever. But she had opened up to Finn, and instead of running away from her, he'd held on tighter. She didn't ever want him to let go. She closed her eyes, and as she drifted off to sleep, Finn's hand wrapped around hers.

Melody woke what must have been a few hours later, this time alone on the couch, the aroma of freshly brewed coffee filling the air. She sat up groggily, pushing the hair from her eyes. The fire was roaring, and suddenly Finn was standing in front of her, holding two mugs of coffee and a smile that made her want to keep him forever.

He sat down beside her, giving her a quick kiss and coffee. He'd already showered, and she smiled at him before taking a sip of coffee. "Thank you. What time is it?"

"Ten."

She gasped. "What?"

He laughed. "I know. We're wasting our last day of peace sleeping."

She scrambled to her feet and looked down at his handsome face. "I'm going to shower, and then we're going to make the most of this day."

"You know, when you declared that we were going to make the most of this day together, I naively thought we were on the same page," Finn grumbled. "Standing on a ladder and stringing Christmas lights is not my idea of making the most of today."

Melody swallowed her laugh and handed him the rest of the lights. Snow flurries trickled down, and the storm had passed. The roads were still closed, but the sun had come out and made the air not feel quite so cold. Or maybe it was Finn. Despite his complaints, she knew he was having fun. These days with him had been the best days of her life. There was this thrilling freedom in being with him. She had never felt so much like herself. "We're almost done. Think how excited Isabella will be to see all the lights. Seriously. Then all we have left to do is make a snowman."

Finn swore under his breath. "A snowman? Shouldn't she be doing that? We're adults—we don't have to build snowmen."

Melody stared up at him and shrugged. He paused,

something flickering over his eyes as he turned to look down at her. She should tell him. She took a deep breath and leaned into that feeling of trust that was growing with him. "I've never really…built a snowman. No time. Addie would. Every time there was a fresh snowfall, she'd be out there in the front yard, building some adorable snowman. And every time, when she would come back inside, instead of receiving a nice cup of hot chocolate and praise, our mom would ridicule her. She told her that she was wasting her time on stupidities and she should try and be more like me and Molly."

Finn finished attaching the last light, his expression stony before climbing down the ladder. Her heart was racing because she felt silly telling him all this stuff that shouldn't matter as a grown-up. Instead, he stood in front of her and then leaned forward and kissed the spot just below her ear, and she grabbed onto his forearms. His mouth lingered there, and her knees were wobbly as he whispered against her neck, his lips brushing against her skin. "Then let's build the best damn snowman ever. Lucky for you, I'm an expert. But that means you'll have to take orders. From me."

She was laughing when he kissed her and forgot all about telling him she didn't take orders very well.

An hour later, she was rolling her eyes as Finn lectured her on the importance of mastering the size of the second boulder. "Hey," he said, hands on his lean hips, his eyes sparkling. "No sass for the teacher, please."

She gave him a salute and continued rolling the boulder, coming up with a plan that was so unlike her, unlike anything she'd ever done before, that she knew she had to do it. "Maybe if my teacher wasn't such a know-it-all, I wouldn't have to. You really need to work on your teaching skills. Less bark," she said, keeping her head down so he wouldn't catch her smile.

"I'll try harder," he said with a laugh.

"And what about the hat? The nose? All that stuff," she said, rolling the boulder with more effort now that it had accumulated so much snow. Perfect. She had to stifle her giggle of excitement and then almost paused. She didn't think she'd ever been this giddy in her entire life. Or had ever plotted something so funny. Who was she?

"Amateur. We figure that stuff later."

The smile in his voice made her smile, and as she rolled the boulder to his feet, she stood, dusting the snow off her gloves and looking up at him as innocently as possible. "Is this big enough?"

He glanced at the large boulder they'd made for the base in the center of the front yard and then back to the boulder she'd rolled over. "I guess it'll do for beginners. Not perfect, but it'll do."

She smiled. "I'm so glad. So now what?"

"I'll kneel down and position it. Just be careful as you lift it up. You don't want it to fall apart. It's actually quite a delicate job."

"Yes, definitely. I have no idea how someone like me can manage such a delicate procedure," she said, placing her hands on either side of the perfect boulder.

"Just try your best, sweetheart," he said.

She knew he was baiting her, and that was fine, because she planned on continuing the fun. He stared at her expectantly. "Sure, Finn. Whatever you say, Finn." She picked up the boulder, trying desperately not to give herself away, and at the last moment, instead of placing it on the base of the snowman, she dumped it on Finn's head.

His roar of surprise should have made her run in the opposite direction. But she was laughing too hard at the sight of him covered in snow. The giant boulder of snow had collapsed all over his head, and he looked like he should be in an animated movie. She was going to tell him he reminded her of Olaf, but she kept her mouth shut as he rose slowly to his feet, the gleam in his eyes making her take a step back.

"Melody..."

She swallowed hard and stood her ground. She gave him her sweetest smile. "Yes, Finn?"

"Run."

"Run?" she repeated blankly.

He nodded slowly, taking another step closer to her, his mouth twitching.

She swore under her breath and spun around. She started running as it dawned on her that he was planning on retaliation. She let out a peal of laughter as his hand grazed her jacket before she took off at top speed. "I was the fastest runner in my class," she yelled, heading for the trees, hoping to lose him in that maze.

She sprinted as fast as she could through the deep snow, laughing and huffing as she tried to outrun him. Not hearing him behind her at all after a minute of running, she took a second to glance over her shoulder and slowed down.

She screamed as Finn appeared from one of the trees in front of her and tackled her into one of the giant mounds of fluffy snow. They were both laughing as they landed. He cushioned her fall, and she landed on top of him.

"Let the records show that even with a messed-up leg, I outran you."

She dropped her head and laughed against his neck. "This was payback for Monopoly, wasn't it?"

"No, that'll be later. That was payback for you dumping a pile of snow all over me."

She lifted her head so that she could look into his gorgeous eyes. He cupped her face, icy snow on her cheeks making her yelp. But she forgot all of that as he reached up to kiss her. Soon she was lost in him, in the way he made her feel, in the woman she was with him.

"Finn…what are we going to do tomorrow?"

He rested his forehead against hers and groaned, as though he already knew what she was going to say. "I spent the last hour wondering if it would be really rude to invent some kind of excuse so they wouldn't be able to come. Maybe we have the flu?"

She laughed. "Seriously, though. What *are* we going to do? Are we still going to go through with our plan?"

He sighed. "Seems kind of stupid now…considering."

Her heart raced. "Considering?"

He shrugged, his blue eyes steady on hers. "*Considering* I'm no longer interested in having to fake some kind of breakup, I feel like now, we should do the opposite and pretend we're *not* together, just to piss them off and make them think their plan didn't work."

Melody burst out laughing, a flood of relief and lightness washing over her. "So, what do we do? Pretend like none of this ever happened and they really don't know us at all?"

Finn grinned. "Exactly. All we have to do is pretend for three days. I'm sure we'll have an opportunity to sneak off alone at some point. Three days is a small price to pay so we don't have to watch them gloat. Then, after they've waved good-bye and are out of sight, I'll slam the door shut, and we can get back to *this*," he said, kissing her.

Chapter Ten

Finn shifted slightly, careful not to disturb Melody, who was sleeping, holding onto him like he was her lifeline. And he didn't mind that. He liked that. He liked that she trusted him enough to let her guard down and tell him, without words, that she trusted him. He knew that was huge for her.

Firelight flickered, and the logs on the fire crackled. He figured it was sometime in the middle of the night. They'd both fallen asleep out here, and maybe it'd been intentional because neither of them wanted to go to bed alone, and going to bed together…wasn't an option.

He knew what this was, this warmth that flooded him, that followed him around all day; it was Mel. It was his feelings for her. They had come out of nowhere, had knocked him over, and had him wishing that this could go on forever. The day they'd spent together had been one of the best of his life. He hadn't even minded hanging all the Christmas lights. And that diabolical-looking snowman they'd eventually finished was the greatest thing he'd ever seen. After they'd crafted a wicked expression for the frozen face, he'd run inside to find one of Ben's nicest scarves and hats and had placed it on the snowman. They'd laughed and joked and kissed and kissed some more then walked back into the house, hand in hand.

They'd had hot chocolate and he'd dumped in half the bag of marshmallows and she'd laughed like he was the funniest man in the world. And she made him feel ten feet tall, because making her laugh was just about the best thing.

He'd challenged her to a rematch of Monopoly after they'd prepared and ate dinner, and she'd kicked his ass, despite all his efforts to distract her. She'd even had enough nerve to do a victory dance, which was doubly painful for him to watch. He'd needed a painkiller for his leg after trying to scramble away. That had earned him her sympathy, but he didn't brush it off, because she didn't pity him. He knew the difference. But it was that softer side of herself that she showed him…that made him hurt for her, for everything she'd been through, for everything she'd kept hidden from the world because she was afraid it would be used against her. He wanted so much more than that for her.

He also wanted more days like they'd just had. More days to be *them*.

She sighed and placed her hand over his heart, her eyes still shut. He forced himself to close his eyes and placed his hand over hers. He suddenly didn't know anything anymore, except that he didn't want to share her with anyone. He didn't want anyone intruding on this safe place they'd created for themselves. But he knew their family…tomorrow everything would change.

• • •

Melody peered out the window, looking for any signs of their family. All she saw was a clear blue sky and sun sparkling off the snow. The tree branches were heavy with all the fresh snow that had fallen, and the outdoors seemed so inviting—even though she knew it had to be freezing out there.

She glanced over at Finn, who was brewing coffee and setting a tray of cinnamon rolls in the oven. She didn't want to share him, but she did agree with his plan. She didn't want anyone intruding on what they were building. This little cabin, which she thought was perfectly adorable and exclusively a place for her equally adorable sister and brother-in-law, had won her heart.

As had the wounded, sweet, gorgeous firefighter who'd run away from life, too. She could be herself with Finn. Yesterday had been the best day of her life. And sleeping on the couch with him, even though it had been cramped, had been the best *sleep* of her life. She'd felt safe. At home. Like everything was right with her world.

But with everyone coming, she was going to have to go back to being the old Melody, the girl who had it all together. She didn't want to be her anymore. That Melody was uptight, so worried about what other people thought of her and what other people thought she should be doing. She had lived life according to her mother's expectations—and she had never met them, no matter how hard she'd tried. That Melody was so hard on herself. She went around thinking she had to project this air of confidence, but on the inside, she was constantly berating herself. It was only last week that she realized that her inner voice was really her mother's voice, repeating everything she'd been told throughout her life. None of it had been good, but it had pushed her to try harder, work harder, and forget the merits of having a life of her own.

"Any sign of them?"

Finn's deep voice cut through her thoughts, and a blanket of warmth settled over her body. She shook her head and turned back around to face him. She wished this was her real life; she wished Finn was hers for real and not just for the holidays. "Is that coffee for us?"

He flashed her a grin that made her toes curl. "You bet," he said, pulling out the carafe and pouring them each a cup.

She joined him in the kitchen and accepted a mug. "Thanks."

His brows drew together. "Hey. You okay?"

She took a sip of the coffee and searched for the words that eluded her. Articulating feelings was not natural for her. She'd suppressed *feeling* her feelings let alone voicing them for so long. And what if he wasn't thinking the same thing?

What if he was looking forward to seeing everyone? Sure, they'd joked about the pressures of appearing happy in front of family, but this went beyond that. She took a deep breath and looked up at him, at that warmth and comfort she'd come to rely on in his green eyes, and just blurted out the truth. "What's going to happen…after all of this?"

Surprise flashed across his eyes…and something else as he took a step closer to her. Her nerves fluttered in her stomach as he reached for her.

The sound of a horn honking repeatedly broke the magic of the moment.

"That is the most obnoxious sound," he said, irritation dripping from his voice.

She sighed. "I know."

"Maybe we can escape out the back door?"

She smiled and remembered how hard she thought it'd be to fake being happy. She wasn't faking. This was the happiest she'd been in her entire life. "So. Friends."

A flicker of something flashed across his eyes. "Right. Friends."

What happened when everyone left? When it was time for her to decide what she was going to do about the Shadow Creek Hospital? When he decided what he was going to do about his own career? He was no longer interested in faking a breakup, but what about the real thing?

Suddenly, everything she'd worked so hard for, everything she thought was so important, seemed to dim in importance… to what she might have found with Finn.

Chapter Eleven

Finn stood beside Melody and plastered a dumb smile across his face as his family piled out of two SUVs like they were starring in a clown skit. How were there so many of them all of a sudden? "Should I go over there and help them unload or pretend my leg is sore and stand here with you?"

Melody let out a choked laugh and nudged him. "I guess we could both go over there. It would be the polite thing to do."

He nodded, watching his brother, who was currently taking instructions from their mom on how to hold the giant gingerbread house he was pulling from the trunk. "True. But it's kind of fun to watch. Oh, look, Ben almost fell in the driveway."

Melody slapped a hand over her mouth, her shoulders shaking.

"No, thanks, we're fine out here!" Ben yelled, making his way toward them, holding the oversize, cellophane-wrapped gingerbread house.

Finn's mom let out a piercing scream. "Finn! Your

beautiful face!"

Ben harrumphed. "I think it looked better before."

Finn rolled his eyes and held out his arms. "Here, give me that. How much did you guys pack, anyway? You don't actually have a baby yet, you know."

"Nice to see you, too. What the hell is that thing on the lawn?" he asked, jutting his chin in the direction of the snowman. "Are you trying to give us nightmares?"

"It's you as a snowman. So…yes."

Ben gave him the finger when their mother wasn't looking. "Hope you're enjoying my rent-free cabin. Hi, Mel," he said, shooting Melody a smile before glaring at Finn.

"It's very nice to see you, too, Ben. But be more careful with this work of art," he said, raising his voice so their mom could hear.

Ben shook his head and walked away. Soon, she and Finn were both being doused in hugs and kisses. He caught Melody's eye over her sister's shoulder, and a pang of longing hit him. Longing for their time together and for whatever it was they were building together.

• • •

"What a wonderful evening this has been!" Finn's mom said with a bright smile as she held up her glass of wine.

Finn smiled. He was happy that she was so happy. She hadn't had the easiest life, and yet she'd always managed to put on a brave face for him and Ben. When their dad died, they had all been devastated. She had never remarried, saying that one soul mate in a lifetime was lucky enough—though he and Ben had noticed the former fire chief and close family friend, Darren Wade, had been hanging around a lot lately. Their mother denied it, but both of them were happy to see her enjoying life again.

The room was filled with all of their roundabout family. Drew and Addie were snuggled on one sofa with their daughter, Isabella, sitting on the rug doing a puzzle. Ben and Molly were on another sofa, his brother on high alert every time Molly put a hand on her stomach. If he hadn't been so preoccupied with his feelings for Melody, he'd be using his brother's anxiety to play amusing pranks for everyone to enjoy. But he didn't have it in him. Because…because he was spending all his time noticing how beautiful Mel was. How she smiled. How she laughed, even at Ben's lame jokes. Then he had to pretend he wasn't watching her. Except he'd catch her watching him, and then he just wanted to kiss her and tell everyone to leave again.

Their time at the cabin together had made him realize how much life he had to live, how the accident hadn't robbed him of who he really was.

"So, when are you coming back to work?" Ben asked as conversation carried on around them. "I can get that physical booked for you."

Shit. He glanced over at his mom, whose smile fell. She hadn't even thought it was a possibility for him. He'd left things very vague because he knew how much she worried. A month ago, there had been no other option for him—get better, get cleared for work, and get back on the job. Now, he wasn't so sure. There were other options. He didn't know if he wanted to go back. But he needed to make sure that he wasn't quitting out of fear, but that his decisions were based on reality. The more he looked into the position of a fire investigator, the more it grew on him. Either way, he'd be disappointing one of them. He had never spoken to Ben about not going back. But he also couldn't get his mother's hopes up that he'd be leaving, either.

He averted his gaze from his mother's and caught Melody looking at him from the kitchen as she made hot chocolate.

"I'm not exactly sure." He kept his voice neutral. He really didn't want to get into this now.

"Yes, Ben, don't pressure him," their mother said.

He leaned forward, resting his forearms on his thighs. "Mom, I have to make my decision by the new year. I can't stay here forever."

His mother stood abruptly, and he caught the faint tremble in her chin. "I'm feeling tired all of a sudden. I think I'll turn in."

He couldn't let her go to bed like this. He stood and followed her out the room, relieved to hear Melody announce that the hot chocolate bar with marshmallows was all set up. He owed her for that one.

"Mom, you okay?"

She turned around sharply, her eyes flashing. "I've been trying to keep my mouth shut, and I can't anymore. I'm so mad at you right now, Finn!"

He shoved his hands in his pockets and leaned against the wall where they stood in the hallway. "I didn't say I was going back for sure. I know you want me to just walk away, and I want to give you what you want so badly, but I can't. It's not that easy. I always thought that I was born to be a firefighter. Like Dad. With Ben." He shook his head and sighed. "It's who we all are, and it scares me to not go back."

Her eyes filled with a rare sighting of tears. "I lost your dad. Then Ben got injured, but you...we almost *lost* you, Finn. I sat by your bed and cried like a baby and prayed with every ounce of strength I had. I talked to your father out loud, begging him not to let you go up there with him. I want you *here* with me. *I* go before you boys. That's what I want. I want to go to bed every night knowing that you boys are safe."

Hell. He walked over to her and hugged her, hating himself. "I'm sorry, Mom. I'm sorry I put you through that. I want to give you what you want, but there are no guarantees.

Even if I had a safe old desk job, something could happen. There is no way to escape it."

But she didn't look relieved. He paused, taking in her appearance. His mother had always been filled with energy, and it felt like half the time she was the one running circles around him and Ben. But not anymore. Her eyes were red, and the lines around them seemed more pronounced. Her laugh lines seemed more like worry lines, and she seemed thinner to him, more fragile.

Guilt ripped through him. He and Ben had always been so determined to follow in their father's footsteps. But maybe now that their mom was getting older, it was harder on her. Tears slipped down her cheeks. "I'm sorry for doing this to you. I'm sorry for being selfish. This will be the one time I ask you—please don't go back. For my sake?"

Her voice was a thin whisper that destroyed him.

He hugged her again, feeling like the most selfish person in the world for doing this to her. "Is that really what you want?"

She covered her face. "No…no. I just want us all to be together for as long as we can. Ben and Molly are going to have this baby, and I want us to enjoy the family getting bigger. I'm sorry. It's not your fault. I'll be fine. I'm always fine. If you decide to go back because it's your calling, then you know I will always support you. It was a moment of weakness. It's… been a heck of a year, Finn. There's more…"

There was more? He braced himself. He didn't want to hear it, but he would never say no to her opening up to him. "Go ahead."

"When I saw you in that ER room? Finn, it brought me back to the night your father died. I sat by his side, I cried, I called his name over and over and wanted him to wake up. He didn't. Just like you didn't that night in the hospital." She held onto him tightly. She felt frail and small in his arms, and his conscience did a number on him. "What if that was your warning? What if that was God telling you it's time to leave this profession?"

He sighed. "I don't think He hands out warnings like that," he said, forcing levity in his tone as he pulled back.

She shook her head and wiped her eyes. "You can make fun of me all you want, but my instincts are telling me it's time for you to find something else."

He reached for her hand. "I would never make fun of you. Maybe tease. Kind of. But I always listen when you speak. Sometimes I have a delayed reaction, but I always value your input."

"Thank you for that. This will be the last time I bring it up. I don't want to guilt you out of doing what you love, even though that's exactly what I'm doing. I just…I needed to tell you. Also, I need to tell you that there is more out there than just firefighting. You are more than a firefighter. You are a good, smart, strong, and very sweet man. Don't think that this has to be your entire life."

He ducked his head. "Thanks, Mom. But I know. I know there's more out there. And trust me when I tell you that I am looking into some other things that might interest me. I don't want to get your hopes up, and I don't want to make promises."

She raised an eyebrow, and all traces of any tears were gone from her now sparkling eyes. She turned and headed into her room. "Fine. Now that we got the more miserable things out of the way, let's move on. I don't want you to miss out on life. I see the looks between you and Melody, Finn. I don't want you to lose out on a future that could be more wonderful than you even imagine."

His stomach dropped as he trailed behind her. Had everyone noticed "the looks?" "Mom, there are no looks, trust me. Also, I'm not Ben. He was in love with Molly forever. It was easy for them to get back together. Those two had basically planned marriage since they met over a decade ago. I barely know Melody, and neither of us are the happily-ever-after, boring people like Molly and Ben, so please don't go getting your hopes up and reading into things that aren't there."

She sat down on the edge of the bed with a theatrical sigh. "There is more to life than work and fun. You don't want your best years to pass you by. You overcame so much this year. There was a time we didn't even know if you'd be walking again, let alone returning to work. Why don't you slow down and really see what you want from life?"

He crossed his arms over his chest and rolled back on his heels. "I know what I want. I want to work. I want to be like the person I was before the accident."

She gave him a half smile that made him feel even guiltier. "Okay, well then who am I to stop you, right? I'm only your mother."

He let out a choked laugh. "You'll never be only my mother. I wouldn't be here right now without you. And you may think all this stubbornness comes from Dad, but I'm pretty sure you're responsible for seventy-five percent of it."

She pursed her lips.

He extended his hand, ready to end this conversation and go back to the safety in numbers. "I love you."

• • •

"All right, now that we're alone, we need an update on the Finn situation," Addie said as they gathered in Melody's room. The guys were in the family room watching *Home Alone* with Finn and Ben's mother Marjorie, and Isabella. Melody frowned at Addie and shut the door quickly.

"There is no situation. Finn is Finn." She flopped on the

bed and reached for her mug of hot chocolate, wishing she'd added some of that brandy to it.

Molly sighed loudly and shook her head. She was seated in the corner chair with her legs propped on the small ottoman. "Are we really going to play this game? Everyone knows something is going on. So we can spend the next ten minutes going back and forth or you can jump to the good stuff right now. What if I go into labor and I still don't know what's happening?"

Melody's stomach dropped. "Don't even joke about going into labor. You have a month to go."

Addie took a sip of hot chocolate. "It's not that big of a deal. It's probably the best-case scenario. Three doctors and two firefighters. You can't get any safer than that."

Of course, Addie or Molly wouldn't get that delivering a baby—her future niece—would be an absolute nightmare for Melody. Like, paralyzing. The pressure of that normally would be crazy, but after what she'd been through, there was no way.

She glanced away from their smiling faces and tried to push those thoughts from her mind. Drew would have to do it. That's all there was to it.

As much as she and Finn joked about having to fake happiness, she didn't feel like she was faking anything anymore. And though she had resented the intrusion on what had become a very special time for her, she was actually having fun.

Their family gatherings had always been so tense growing up and even as adults. Molly rarely attended. She and Addie, when they did attend, were always dying to leave. They'd each have to suffer through a multitude of insults, and though they pretended they were immune to them, they cut deep and let old insecurities ooze through the opening. Only now that the three of them had reunited and worked on their problems did their mother's jabs not matter. Except that voice, the one telling her she wasn't good enough, that she'd never be as smart as Molly or as nice as Addie, hovered around the corner. Addie was the nicest person she ever met and Molly the smartest. She didn't know what that made her. The shrewd one? That wasn't exactly comforting or something to be proud of.

When they were all sitting together at the table earlier, it had felt like she was part of a family that she really loved, and she felt like she truly fit in—the real her.

Sometimes it hurt to look at Molly, like the shame made it hard to really meet her eyes for too long. She didn't deserve her forgiveness.

Molly leaned forward and patted Melody on the hand. "Hey, Mel, we were just joking. I'm not going into labor."

Melody forced a smile. "I should probably be the one reassuring you, not the other way around."

Molly's smile dipped. "What's up with you? I feel like something's off. We were also joking around about the Finn thing, too. *Obviously*, you guys would never work."

Melody sat up a little straighter. "Oh…right. I'm just tired. And of course, Finn and I wouldn't work…because…?"

Addie coughed, covering her face with a pillow. "Sorry, just trying not to spread germs," she said, lying horribly.

"That's my pillow," Melody said.

Addie threw it to the other side of the room, her face beet red. "Sorry."

"So, you guys were saying? About me and Finn?" She fidgeted with the handle of her mug.

"Nothing. It's just that you're such different personality types." Molly shrugged. "He's so easygoing and stuff."

She wanted to say that they didn't know Finn the way she did. He had this deep, soulful side to him that made her feel safe and understood. Maybe the most understood she'd ever felt in her entire life. But if she said that, she'd be betraying his confidence and demonstrating that she really had gotten closer to him. "Well, I guess that's true. He's actually made me question a lot of things. I don't know if I want to come back to the hospital. I've been having a lot of questions and thoughts, and...maybe the hospital isn't right for me anymore," she said, letting it all out. It felt good to confide in them.

Even though they were both staring at her with their mouths hanging open.

"Oh Mel, it's too soon to say that. After everything you've been through," Addie whispered, scrambling off the bed to give her a hug. Melody hugged her back, appreciating the gesture that was so very Addie.

"She's right, Mel," Molly said. "You don't have to rush back. Give it time. Go to counseling."

Melody shrugged. "I've given it more than a week. This is the longest I've ever taken off. Instead of making me want to go back, I feel the opposite. I'm actually getting used to relaxing. I've always been itching to go back after a few days off, but I'm not. I've even learned how to do yoga and meditate. Well. I've *done* yoga and meditation. Not...actually, like, excelled. But I'm trying."

"Still. Maybe it's too soon. I'm glad you're enjoying your time off and you totally deserve it. But what would you do? Hanging out here will get old. You also have to be really honest with yourself. If you want a career change because you hate your job, that's one thing. But running from a really bad day and totally rare situation is another," Molly said gently.

Melody looked away and stood, those nerves she'd forgotten slowly sneaking up on her again, making her muscles tight. "I know. Maybe a few weeks ago, I was running, but now there's more to it. I don't even know if I was ever supposed to be a doctor. Maybe I'm just a doctor because Mom shoved that down my throat my entire life. What if I have something I'm really good at that I don't know about?" She stared at the marshmallows bobbing in the hot chocolate.

"You're a really great doctor," Addie said. "I don't think you're giving yourself any credit for what you've achieved. You wouldn't have gotten to where you are if it was only because Mom pushed you."

"I wish I could stay in this cabin in the middle of nowhere forever," she said without even thinking about filtering her thoughts. She was pretty sure that looks were being exchanged. The old Melody would never have said any of this.

"You can stay here as long as you want, and you can come back here whenever you want. But you can't run from life, Mel. Every doctor has a horror story, something they wish they could go back and change or look at from a different angle. I went into the hospital yesterday to get a few things from my office now that I'm officially on maternity leave and…I heard. You should have told me. What happened to that woman was not your fault," Molly said gently.

Melody's eyes filled with tears, but she kept her gaze on the serene view of the forest out the window. "I don't know if I'll ever get over the guilt. I felt her sadness to my core. I can't shake it."

"That's what makes you a good doctor. You're compassionate and dedicated, and you truly want what's best for your patients. You haven't been faking it all these years. Maybe you are too hard on yourself."

Maybe she wasn't hard enough on herself. Maybe she needed to get it all out there and see what they thought of her if they knew the truth. Would that be selfish? It was almost Christmas, and Molly was pregnant. Her sister had worked so hard at finding her happiness and putting the past behind her. Did she really need to be dragged down into the memories of their childhood?

"What else is going on with you, Mel?" Addie asked,

breaking the silence.

Melody took a deep breath and turned to face them, her gaze going back and forth, along with her rationale. No, she needed to tell Molly. They both needed to know and then maybe they really could move on and their relationship could be even better because it was all out in the open. "I um, I've been holding onto a lot of...shame and regret, and I feel like...no, I *know* I haven't been the best sister to either of you. But you in particular, Molly."

Molly frowned. "What are you talking about? You are both the best sisters, ever."

Melody shook her head and stared at the ground. Her stomach churned and her heart raced. "I have always been so jealous of you. Not now—now, I'm only happy for you. But growing up, I was obsessed with doing better than you at everything. There were times..." She covered her face as a sob hit her. What was happening to her? It was this stupid happy cabin. It was like she was making up for the years of repressing all her emotions.

"Hey, it's okay," Molly said softly.

She took a shaky breath, willing herself to focus and get this over with. *Get it together, Mel.* "I know now it was all to get Mom's approval. She would always compare me to you and tell me I would never be as smart as you...and she told me that I was like her. That I put my own needs above others and that was my one good quality. And it started happening. I *did* do that. And I broke your snow globe on purpose," she said, this time not hiding her tears from Molly.

Molly reached forward and grabbed her hand, squeezing hard. "I know. I know you did, and I know why you did it. You should have had that snow globe. I hated that she made you feel bad and made you feel like you were never good enough. I spent a long time in therapy, and I realized then just how badly she hurt all of us. I'm so grateful to have you and Addie as my sisters, and I regret the years I spent hiding from you. We can't go and change the past and the decisions we made, but we have control over what we do right now. The kind of sisters we want to be, the kind of family we want to be. We can't let Mom take any more away from us. You have to let go; you have to forgive yourself."

Molly hugged her the best she could with her pregnant belly. Addie joined in from behind, and for the first time in… forever, Melody felt the weight of her past slowly lift.

"You two are the best," she managed to whisper.

Chapter Twelve

Finn heard Melody's bedroom door click shut, followed by the sound of footsteps, and glanced at the clock on his nightstand. Five in the morning. Perfect. No one would be awake this early on Christmas morning except Mel. He had a feeling she was going down to the gym. He dressed quickly and used the bathroom, stopping to look at his shaven face. Ugh. Family.

After his mother's heartbreaking conversation last night, he'd been craving his space again. No, not really. He'd been craving Melody. Talking to her, listening to her, kissing her. All this family was too intrusive. He hadn't had a decent conversation alone with her since they'd arrived. He never realized how much he could miss a person who was in the same room. Having a house filled with family was turning out to be even more demanding than he'd anticipated.

He quickly and quietly left his room, relieved to see the lights were off everywhere. He made his way downstairs and opened the gym door.

Melody was standing on the treadmill and gave him a

gorgeous smile that made his heart pound and blood rush through him. He shut the door, turned off the lights, and walked toward her, his gaze not leaving hers. "I missed you," he said thickly as he pulled her into him.

She slid her arms up his chest. "Me, too."

He kissed her like he hadn't seen her in a year because that's what it felt like. "I wish they'd all go home," he said in between kisses.

She laughed softly against his mouth. "I know. How much longer? Are they leaving tonight or tomorrow?"

His hands slid into the nape of her neck and he kissed her deeply—until the lights turned on, jarring them both.

They turned in the direction of the door. Ben was standing there, his mouth hanging open. "Hell. I *knew* it. Normally, I'd have a field day with this, but we don't have time," he said, running his hands through his hair. His eyes were rimmed with red and his hair was messy.

"It's five o'clock in the morning," Finn snapped. "What could you possibly want?"

"It's Molly. She's in labor."

Oh, crap. Melody dug her fingers into his arm. Finn thought she might throw up. Or pass out. Her face had gone from a beautiful flush to green in five seconds. He grabbed one of her hands, hoping she'd focus on him and not give into the panic. "Are you sure?" he asked his brother. Her hand felt clammy in his, and she was clutching him like a lifeline.

Ben gave a nod, his gaze going from Finn to Melody. "Positive. I know it's early, but this will be okay. The baby was always measuring big. I've already called in for an ambulance, but the roads are bad, and we're looking at a few hours if we're lucky. We're going to have to prepare for a home-bath scenario. Mel, can you come upstairs?"

Melody opened her mouth, but only a small gust of air came out. Shit. He knew she was terrified.

"Yeah. Just, uh, give her a minute, Ben," he said when she made no motion to go anywhere.

He was relieved when she finally nodded.

He turned to her when Ben left the room. "I can't do this, Finn," she said, her voice a thin whisper.

Sympathy for her flooded him, but he knew he couldn't show her. He couldn't let her wallow in her fear. He gently but firmly grasped her shoulders. "You have no choice, babe. You are the only OB/GYN here, and you're brilliant and capable."

She shut her eyes briefly. "Drew. He's a great ER doctor. He's delivered so many babies. He's much more qualified. He's smarter, more reliable." Her voice came in choppy breaths. "Get Drew."

He squeezed her shoulders and crouched slightly to meet her gaze. "You are all of those things if not more. This is your area of expertise. Molly is your sister. That is our niece inside her, Melody. You can't let her down," he said, trying to keep the panic from his voice while being understanding. But he knew he couldn't let her flounder. He knew she would regret this for the rest of her life if she didn't deliver Molly's baby.

Her eyes welled with tears. "Finn, I *can't* do it. What if something goes wrong? That baby isn't due for another month."

"You heard Ben; the baby is big. It's not even an entire month early."

"Great, she's going to have a giant baby. At home. Why do you guys have to be so giant?" She rubbed her temples. "This is all Ben's fault."

He couldn't help but chuckle. "You like us giant. Anyway, an ambulance is on the way. She might not even have the baby here. She could be in labor for hours and hours, right?"

This time an actual sob broke loose, and he drew her into his arms because he couldn't stand seeing her like this. "It's not her first baby. This is so bad, Finn. There are so many things you don't know, and this isn't the time to tell you. But that baby…she is so desperately wanted, and I can't be trusted to be the one to bring her into this world. I can't."

He pulled back and cupped her face in his hands, trying to will some confidence into her and give her the harsh truth. "Stop it. You can. You have done tough things before, and you can do them again. Think back way past that last delivery. Think back to all the deliveries that were high risk. Think back to all the things that went wrong that you somehow made right. Do it," he said when she opened her mouth to protest, his voice sounding harsh.

She squeezed her eyes shut and nodded.

He held his breath, and then she opened her eyes a minute later, some of the panic leaving. "You're a human being, right? As dedicated, brilliant, and knowledgably as you are, you don't have the ultimate control over your life or anyone's. Shit happens. Shit happens that we can't control, no matter how hard we try, how perfectly we do something. It took me a long time to realize that, Mel. I replayed my accident over and over. What I could have done, what I should have done, and you know what? I would have done it all the same the next time. But shit happened. I fell. Circumstances that were beyond my control took over. So, same for you. Think back to that delivery. Was there really something you could have done that would have saved that baby's life? Was it really your fault?"

She bit her lower lip and slowly shook her head. "No," she said softly before throwing her arms around his neck.

He held her close to him, pride for her running through his body. He knew how hard it was to let go of guilt and to trust in yourself again. He kissed the top of her head. "I believe in you. You can do this. Everyone upstairs believes in you. No one has ever doubted or questioned you. No one is as hard on you as you are on yourself. So, go up there, be there for your sister, and bring our niece into the world." He leaned down to kiss her.

She kissed him back, and he knew this was more than a pep talk. He knew she was more than the girl he'd had a good time with at the cabin. He was falling for her. She was incredibly brave and strong and brilliant. And he wanted her. Long after the holidays. And the thought of that didn't even terrify him.

"Thank you," she whispered, pulling back.

He gave her another quick kiss and took her hand, walking toward the door. "You're welcome."

She was looking confident again, her eyes clear and sharp. "I've got my hospital bag in the trunk."

"I'll get it for you. Whatever you need in there, I've got your back."

"Okay. This is going to be okay," she said as they left the gym, sounding like she was speaking to herself more than him.

"It will. Deliver that baby, then maybe they'll all leave so we can concentrate on us again. I plan to show you exactly how amazing I think you are," he said, flashing her a smile as they made their way up the stairs.

She blushed a little. "Thank you, Finn. Thank you for believing in me."

...

Melody stared into her sister's eyes, and before even saying a word, she knew Molly was freaking out. "Hey, it's going to be okay," Melody said, squeezing Molly's hand. She was in control again, and Drew was going through their medical bags and telling Ben what else they would need. Addie, Finn, and Marjorie were all in the great room, ready to help with anything. Ben, unfortunately, looked like he was doing even worse than Molly.

"Mel, I have to tell you something. As of my last appointment with the midwife, my baby is breech. She had attempted to turn her but so far nothing."

Melody blinked, trying to appear like this wasn't a big deal, when she really just wanted to scream. It *was* a big deal. Melody schooled her features as her gaze went from Molly's to Drew's concerned one. They knew the stats. If you were delivering in a hospital with a doctor, a breech baby was going to mean a C-section most likely. Neither she nor Drew were experienced in delivering a breech baby in a home setting. "Okay, that's okay."

"I wanted to have this baby at home, but now..."

She soaked in the fear in Molly's eyes and didn't want to be the doctor anymore. She just wanted to be her sister. She knew why Molly didn't want to have the baby in the hospital. She knew why Molly had opted for a midwife and doula, and she fully supported her. Even though she and Molly were both doctors, even though they both believed in what they did at the hospital, the midwife and doula were what Molly needed. But Molly's memories of her first delivery and everything surrounding it were too traumatic. She wanted this experience to be radically different.

Melody blinked rapidly, refusing to give into her emotions. An essential part of this was going to be confidence. Molly had to have confidence in herself and in Melody and Drew as well. She glanced up at Ben, who was whiter than the sheets. "All of us are here for you. We can do this. But you have to believe it, too. Your little girl has a strong heartbeat. We have an ambulance en route, but I have a feeling you'll be holding your baby girl before they get here. Ben, can you get me the midwife's number?" she said, starting to feel that old familiar adrenaline and confidence kick in.

Ben nodded, pulling out his phone and finding the

contact. "Here, just take my phone," he said, handing it to her before sitting on the bed next to Molly and kissing her.

Melody turned to Drew. "Drew and I are going to consult quickly and be right back, okay?"

"We'll be right outside," Drew added, opening the door.

Everyone stared at them as they emerged from the bedroom. She had a hard time avoiding Finn's stare and almost didn't want to meet his gaze, but when she finally did, his eyes were glittering with confidence in her, and she took a deep breath.

"Let's go to the porch. I think the fresh air is a good idea," Drew said.

Marjorie stepped forward, ringing her hands. Addie had her arm around her. "How is Molly?"

Melody forced a smile. "She's great. We just need to discuss a few things and we'll be right back in there."

A minute later, she was thankful for the cool air outside because she felt like she was overheating. She briefed Drew, and they spent the next few minutes sharing their opinions of the best way to go about the delivery. "I'm just going to call her midwife before I get back in there. I need to know as much as I can about Molly and how she'd approach this delivery."

"Okay, I'll stay with Molly." He gave her a reassuring smile. "It's going to be okay, Mel."

She gave him a nod and dialed the midwife, spending the next several minutes gathering as much knowledge as she could. Thankfully, she was very helpful and would be on standby to offer her help over the phone during the delivery if needed. Melody walked to the edge of the porch and lifted her face to the sky. Winter wind blasted her face, and she sent up some fervent prayers for Molly and the baby, and one for herself—to be the doctor her sister needed her to be.

Melody marched back into the house a few moments

later with laser focus. She could do this. When she walked back into the bedroom, the terror in Ben and Molly's eyes almost stopped her in her tracks. The panic there was enough to make her want to run, but she couldn't. She would never. At least she knew now that under the worst circumstances, she could count on herself. She would never run from anyone who needed help, especially not her sister.

She would do whatever it took to get this baby into the world. She grasped Molly's hand and knelt beside her. "Do you trust me?"

Molly squeezed her eyes shut and nodded. "It's not you… don't think it's you… Mel, I can't lose this baby," she said as a sob broke from her, the sound so gut-wrenching like it was coming from somewhere so deep inside, a well of wishes so deep that had never come to fruition.

"We're not," Ben said harshly. "Everything is going to be okay."

"He's right," Melody said, squeezing Molly's hand.

"We won't let anything happen to either of you," Drew chimed in.

"But we all have to work together. There's no time or room for any of us to panic, okay? You have to focus. We all have to focus. Your midwife is on standby. She can guide us through the whole thing. I can get her on the phone if you want?"

She caught the tears in Ben's eyes, the ashen face, the clenched jaw, and knew he was struggling to keep it together for Molly. Molly took a deep breath. "I trust you."

"Okay, then we're going to do this exactly how she would have, exactly like you planned. Pretty soon, you'll be holding your little girl, okay?"

Melody didn't make promises lightly. And after the last delivery, she never wanted to make one again. But today she had to. She had to come through.

Chapter Thirteen

Finn paced the room, walking his laps in the opposite direction of his mother's. Poor Addie, he had no idea how she was dealing with the two of them. Thankfully, Isabella was watching *Frozen 2* in Drew and Addie's room and had no inclination that anything was wrong.

Hours had gone by. Hours and hours with Drew coming out only twice to tell them everything was going well but slow. Like that was reassuring for anyone.

Addie appeared a moment later, holding two mugs. He and his mother stopped walking, on opposite sides of Addie. "You both need to drink this," she said.

He took the cup and frowned at it. "Thanks, but what the hell is this?"

She shot him a smile. "It has chamomile in it. To relieve some of the stress."

His mother plucked both mugs from their hands. "Addie, you know I love you like family, but we need coffee. Caffeine. Reinforcements. We could be up all night," she said, marching to the kitchen.

Addie turned around, clearly alarmed. "Are you sure that's wise? You haven't eaten anything all day. Don't you think another pot of coffee will only add to your—"

She stopped speaking when an unmistakeable, beautiful, wonderful newborn baby's cry pierced the quiet cabin.

The three of them looked at each other, and damn if they all didn't cry.

He turned around and wiped his face on his shirt sleeve before his mother bulldozed into him for a hug. He held onto her. Relief and joy like he'd never experienced pummeled through him, robbing him of all thought. He just felt. Sheer joy. For all of them. For Molly and Ben, who'd been to hell and back with their relationship and had the courage to keep dreaming and were now being rewarded with a baby with a healthy set of lungs. And for his mother, who had put up with all the stress of their professions to now be rewarded with a grandchild. And for Mel, who had proven to herself that she was not a quitter. He opened his arm, and Addie came in for a group hug.

The door opened many long minutes later, and his big brother walked into the room, unabashedly crying like a baby and holding his little girl. He wanted to make a joke and tell him to hold her up like Simba but couldn't. He was too busy trying not to cry again as Ben walked over.

Finn found himself smiling down at the cutest baby ever.

"She's the most beautiful baby I have ever seen," their mother declared.

"Molly's good?" Finn asked, his voice hoarse.

Ben nodded. "She's amazing."

He glanced in the direction of the room, pride coursing through him as he heard Melody's soft voice speaking with Drew. He knew what this meant for her. So much. More than anyone here would know. She had brought their niece into the world and had conquered her fears at the same time.

"I've got to go back and be with Molly," Ben said, taking the baby from their mom.

"Tell her we love her and we'll be waiting right here. Whatever you need, you've got it," she said.

Ben nodded and gave her a quick kiss on the cheek before turning to go back into the room. Finn turned to his mother, finding his sense of humor again. "So how does it feel, Granny?"

She smacked him on the arm. "I told you, I'm Grandmaman."

He laughed. "We're not French. I think Granny has a nice ring to it," he said, enjoying teasing her now that everything was okay.

Her eyes narrowed. "You can call me Granny when you come home and restart your life."

He made a mental note to make that happen ASAP.

...

Melody burst out of the bedroom, elation and joy and gratitude pummelling through her body. There was only one person she needed to see, and she didn't even care who saw. Her gaze found him immediately, and it was as though everything stopped.

For her, that moment, the expression in Finn's eyes, was something that she'd never experienced. No one had ever looked at her with that kind of pride, that kind of love. And even though most of their family was in the room, she ran to him, and he wrapped her up into his arms.

He held her to him, his face buried in her neck. "I knew you could do it. I'm so proud of you."

She didn't want the moment to end. It was the first time in her life she felt truly accepted, with flaws and all. She didn't have to pretend to be perfect or to have it all together. He believed in her when she didn't even believe in herself. He hadn't even batted an eye. He'd known she could do it. He slowly lowered her to the ground and smiled.

Reality slowly set in as she looked up at him, at his gorgeous face. "They are all staring at us, aren't they?"

He leaned forward and kissed her softly. "Yup. Addie actually just took a picture."

She swallowed her laugh. "Can we disappear?"

"I'll see what I can do," he said with a soft chuckle then announced, "We just need to get some fresh air."

Addie gave her a wave and smug smile. Melody almost laughed as she remembered their conversation the night before. Finn held open the door and grabbed his coat.

He placed it around her shoulders as the cold wind greeted them on the porch. "Aren't you cold?" she asked.

He shook his head. "I was dying in there. You did it, Mel," he said, leaning down and giving her a quick kiss.

She nodded. "I did. Finn, I didn't think I was going to be able to. We didn't want to worry your mom, so we didn't say anything, but the baby was breech. And big. And a C-section wasn't an option here…I mean, I know I was the most qualified, but I was…I was so scared."

He let out a rough sigh. "Oh man, that's brutal."

She nodded. "I wanted to run away. Obviously, I had to just do it. Drew was great. So calm under pressure. He was the perfect person to have by my side. We had her midwife on the phone, and she was fantastic. Of course, your brother was phenomenal and knew exactly how to give Molly what she needed. And as usual, Molly was amazing. I don't know where she gets her strength from, but after the panic gave way, she became laser focused and did exactly as we told her."

He pulled her into his arms, and the sound of sirens in the distance cut through the otherwise silent night. "I'm so happy for you and for them."

"There's something else I had never counted on. I mean, first thing was that I was so happy and so grateful to be holding that little girl. Our niece. Molly and Ben's perfect little baby. But then this other emotion just came out of nowhere—I knew I was right where I was supposed to be. I was *meant* to deliver that baby. I was meant to do this *job*. It wasn't about impressing my mother. Or it hasn't been for a very long time. I love what I do. I love bringing these new little people into the world and handing them over to their parents. There is no doubt in my mind anymore," she said, the relief almost making her feel light-headed.

He kissed her and drew back when the sirens became louder. "I'm so happy for you. There's that ambulance. Finally."

"We should let them know," she said, holding his hand. It was like all the weight she'd been carrying around the last month had lifted, and not only did she know that she'd be going back to the hospital, she knew that she wasn't a fraud. She loved her job, she loved her life, and she loved the person she was turning into.

"Maybe that means everyone will clear out to go to the hospital?" he said with an adorable half smile. She stared at him, knowing he was a part of all this and this setup by their siblings had been the best intrusion they'd ever made into her life.

"Nope. Addie and Isabella and Drew will be here," Ben said, holding the door open for them.

Finn frowned at him. "Aren't you supposed to be with your wife and baby?"

Ben grinned. "I thought I heard sirens so thought I'd come out and check."

They walked back in the house and stood to the side as the paramedics came in, and soon, they were all waving Molly and Ben and the baby off.

There was nothing that could take the joy out of the room as they all stood there.

A Christmas baby.

There was a new baby in their family, a new person to love and cherish, and as she looked around at everyone's smiling faces, she knew that this was what she'd been missing out on. She had turned people away, family away, relationships away because she'd been so busy proving to the world who Melody Mayberry really was. But she wasn't any of those things. She was *this* woman. The one that was loved by these people and accepted by them. She didn't have to be any more than who she was right now.

They walked back inside and helped pack up everyone's things and saw them off. The house seemed extra quiet as the door shut. "Best Christmas ever," Melody said, smiling up at Finn.

He leaned down to kiss her. "I have something. Hold on." He walked over to the tree and picked up a small red box.

Her heart tripped in panic. "Wait, we didn't say we were exchanging gifts."

He gave her a lopsided grin and held out the box. "I know."

She accepted the gift, holding his gaze, falling for him just a little more. Since their family had arrived, there was so much drama and so much emotion that she was exhausted. But so alive. She didn't want to go to sleep because she didn't want to miss out on life. She'd done that for too long. Finn was so much of the reason.

Melody stared at the gorgeous ribbon on the box, unable to move it, not knowing what to say. "Finn, I didn't get you anything. I mean, how did you even have time to buy something? I feel so bad. I can't take this." She tried to shove the box at him.

He just laughed and kissed her. "Just open it. I know we

didn't plan on exchanging gifts. It's little. Don't worry."

Her chest squeezed at the sparkle in his eyes and she pulled one of the ribbons until it opened. She gave him a glance before opening the lid on the box. She gently pushed aside the tissue and gasped. Tears blurred her vision, and goose bumps filled her arms as she slowly pulled out the snow globe. "How did you know?"

"I saw you holding the globe at the store, and you had this faraway look on your face. I just knew it was important to you somehow."

"I can't believe you did this," she said softly, turning it over and back upright. Just as it always did, the little idyllic scene inside filled her with a longing for the life it depicted. She wanted that. She wanted to be like those people. Maybe even more now that she knew life didn't have to be perfect in order to be great. And people didn't need to be perfect in order to do amazing things.

"Merry Christmas," he said, leaning forward to kiss her softly.

"I don't know how I'll ever thank you for everything. My time here. I never expected…any of this. You. I never expected you to be so great."

He gave a short laugh. "What did you think I was?"

She smiled. "I didn't think at all. I didn't think about anything other than work. And proving myself. So, when I failed or when something went wrong, I crumbled. I came here trying to escape life, but you are the most life I have ever experienced."

"I'm glad. I'm flattered. And you know I came up here to escape, too. But I don't want to hide out here anymore. I want to go back to Shadow Creek. And I want you to come with me."

Chapter Fourteen

Melody stared at Finn, her heart racing. "With you?"

He gave her a nod, taking a step closer to her.

Her phone vibrated, the sound jarring in the quiet room. "I don't want to answer it, but I should. It could be the hospital about Molly. One of the doctors might have questions."

"Of course, get it," Finn said.

She dashed across the room to grab it off the counter. The screen didn't show a number or name. "Hello?"

Finn's phone also rang, and she indicated she'd be in the bedroom so she could hear better. He gave her a nod and answered his own phone. Shutting the door behind her, she continued to just hear static. And then the unmistakeable sound of her mother's voice. "Melody, is that you? I can barely hear you."

Why was her mother calling her now? She forced herself to answer. "Yes, I can hear you now."

"Well, Merry Christmas to you, too. You know this call is practically a thousand dollars a minute from the cruise ship, but I needed to get a hold of you. The other day, I was at the hospital for my annual mammogram—no thanks to either of my daughters who are doctors who fail to ever remind me to get this test done—and I happened to run into your boss, Cadence Winthrop."

Melody's stomach dropped. Her mother never "ran into" anyone by accident. Bulldozed into people was more like it. But even then, Melody knew Cadence was very professional and would never tell her mother anything. There were confidentiality rules. "So?" she snapped, hating that her mother was already succeeding at pushing all her buttons. This had been the best day of her life up until now.

"I can see you're already getting your back up. Anyway, there are rumors of a lawsuit."

Melody broke out into a cold sweat, and acid swirled in her stomach. A lawsuit. She shut her eyes. That couple—they *did* blame her. Oh, God. A lawsuit. An investigation? No one would trust her again. She would have to defend herself, and that was the last thing she wanted right now. She could barely defend herself to herself. She could barely stand to look in the mirror up until today. "I didn't…I didn't know," she finally managed to whisper.

"See, aren't you glad I care so much that I'm making this call from the Caribbean? Now, here's my advice to you: leave the hospital. Yes, you'll still have to go through the investigation, but at least you won't have to suffer the humiliation of being in a small town and having people stare or, worse, ask hurtful questions. You won't have to watch your patient list dwindle as word spreads around town. I suggest going back to the city where you'll be in a big hospital. You'll get patients out of sheer need, and no one there will associate you with the lawsuit unless they really dig deep. You'll be able to start over, free of scandal."

Melody felt like she was going to throw up. She slowly leaned against the door for support and lowered herself to the floor. Everything was clammy, and the acid rose up uncontrollably. Leave town. Humiliation. Scandal? Everyone would think it was all her fault that baby died. She covered her face and tried taking deep breaths. She couldn't lose it. She didn't have panic attacks. She was calm and collected under pressure.

"Melody, are you there?"

Maybe she could just pretend she wasn't. But then her mother would just call her back. No, the only way to get her off the phone would be to agree with her. Though that may be her only way out of this mess. Her mother may actually be right. "I'm here. Thank you for your information and your advice. I'll, uh…I'll start making arrangements."

"Good. See that you do. I only have your best interests at heart, you know that. You were the one who always saw the world the way I did, Melody. If you only had Molly's intelligence, we could have been the best of friends. Do say hello to your sisters for me…and my sons-in-law who clearly want nothing to do with me either. I'm assuming you all had a wonderful Christmas together. But don't worry, I'm not hurt. I'll talk to you soon."

Melody ended the call and held her face in her hands as nausea overwhelmed her. How could this be happening? Everyone would know. And Finn. He was waiting for her. She couldn't tell him this—he wouldn't understand. He would tell her to stay strong and fight. But she didn't want that. She didn't want to have to live in Shadow Creek and face everyone while all this was happening. She didn't want pity or hate.

Get yourself together, Mel.

She took a few deep breaths and scrambled to stand, adrenaline running through her. She pulled her suitcase out from under the bed and opened it. She had to leave.

Melody crammed her clothes into her suitcase, not even caring that everything would be wrinkled when she unpacked. None of it mattered.

She couldn't face Finn right now. He didn't need to be dragged into her mess; he needed to concentrate on getting his own life back.

Maybe if she was lucky, he wouldn't be waiting for her in the living room and she could escape like a coward and text him later. She was planning on slipping away like a thief in the night and going to see Cadence at the hospital first thing tomorrow. She needed to hear it from her and then resign. She could at least spare Cadence the disgrace of having a doctor who was being sued at the hospital. Then her plan was to text Addie and Molly once she'd left town. It would be fine. Once she was settled back in the city, she would call them and explain what happened. She would never let the distance that had happened before repeat itself. But that didn't mean she had to see them every single day in order to be close.

But her heart was already breaking at not seeing at least one of them most days of the week. And her niece. She wasn't going to be able to see her grow up. Or Isabella. She zipped her suitcase shut. That's what pictures were for.

So her only other problem was Finn. But she couldn't risk her entire career on a guy she'd fallen for over the holidays. What if it was just this place? What if when they were back in Shadow Creek, he realized she wasn't the one for him—especially with the hot mess she was in now. It's not like he'd declared his undying love for her. That kind of whirlwind romance didn't happen to her. Just because she'd fallen for him didn't mean there was happily ever after waiting for her. She wasn't that likeable or loveable. She was okay with that. She had always been okay with that. Until Finn.

Pulling her suitcase off the bed, she took a quick survey of the room, making sure she had all her belongings. Time to go. She placed her hand on the doorknob, ready to yank it open, and then stopped herself.

Wait. What was she doing? Running away?

That's what the old Mel would have done. She couldn't do that to Finn. She owed him more than that—she owed him the truth. Ignoring the tremble in her hand, she slowly opened the door, not really knowing what she was going to say, but willing to take the risk.

"Everything okay?"

Melody jumped at the sound of Finn's deep voice. Her eyes adjusted to the dim lighting to find him standing behind the island pouring two glasses of wine. The fireplace flickered and crackled, and the house was the way it was before their family had arrived. They'd shared secrets here, she'd become another woman here, and now she was running away from all of it. She forced a smile as she rolled her suitcase to the door. Her heart was racing, and that sick feeling that had permeated her body when she was speaking to her mother settled into her stomach again. "I was coming out to find you."

He crossed the room, hesitating when he spotted her suitcase, and gently grabbed her hand. "What's going on, Mel?"

The tenderness in his voice made the back of her eyes sting as she looked up at his handsome face. *Just tell him the truth. That's what people do.* She shrugged. "It was my mom on the phone."

He frowned. "Okay…?"

She clutched his hand tightly, reminding herself that he was the man who'd believed in her without even knowing her. "I'm trying so hard to be honest, Finn. I…my mom said that the couple…they may be suing me," she choked out. Her mother's words and disappointment engulfed her in shame, and she stood there, unable to meet his gaze. But he didn't say anything except pull her into him and held onto her tightly. She dug her nails into his back, his silent, unconditional support giving her everything she needed. Everything that had been missing her entire life.

"It's going to be okay. If your mom is actually telling the truth—which I'm not convinced she is, after what you've told me this week—this will be okay. *You* will be okay. It wasn't your fault." He pulled back and framed her face in his hands. His blue eyes were steely, his jaw set.

"I want to believe that so badly," she said, biting back a sob.

"Then believe it. You have to. You can't run from this. You have to defend yourself, Mel."

She shut her eyes and nodded. "I know. I just…I feel so ashamed and so stupid. Like maybe I've just been a sham all these years. I need to go back to the hospital and get some answers."

He gave her a nod. "Okay. I think that's a good idea. You can't leave now, though. It's late. Those roads are crappy at the best of times in the winter."

She shrugged. "I'll take it slow."

"Give me a couple minutes to pack up my things. I'll go with you."

Ugh. How could he be such a great guy? Finn had turned out to be everything she'd ever imagined and so much more without even trying. She shook her head and forced a smile. There was no way she was going to drag him down with her. He'd spend his time defending her and not dealing with his own career. She already couldn't handle the shame—it would be way worse with him there because what if in the end he left her? It was better for her to end things now. "I'll be fine. Um, I will, uh, text you when I know more. I need to do this on my own."

His brows snapped together. "What? Why? At least let me come with you."

He was being so sweet. She'd never had someone around when she had a problem. It was her own fault, because she'd never gotten close enough to anyone to tell them about her problems. And she assumed that everyone would judge her as harshly as her mother. Right now, the idea of letting Finn go with her and seeing her at her worst was something she couldn't quite deal with. "I need to do this on my own."

"Well, I get that. I'm not going to follow you into the hospital. Just let me drive you back. Let me be there for you."

She pulled her hand from his and crossed her arms over her chest. She couldn't do that—because if she was fired or if she found out she was being sued, she'd be too embarrassed to see him. And if it was all true...she didn't know what that meant for her life in Shadow Creek. "This is my problem. I made this mistake by myself, and I need to deal with it by myself. This is all too much. My mom, the family, the pressure at work. And you and I will be such a distraction for each other. You might be taking your career in a whole new direction, and I won't be able to focus..." Her voice trailed off. It was so lame. Her excuse was cold and petty and just like the person she was when she entered this cabin two weeks ago. That person would have pushed aside almost anyone for her career.

He ran his hands through his hair. "I don't buy that for a second. I know you want me to, but why? Why won't you trust me?"

She searched his eyes for something he wouldn't be able to give her, because she wasn't letting him in. Rejection and disappointment from Finn would be even worse than from her mother. What if he *did* begin to doubt her? What if they made her look bad in the trial and, of course, he'd be there, listening? Even if he didn't doubt her, being associated with her—let alone in a relationship with her, if that's where this was headed—would destroy his reputation. There was no way she could do that to him. Not when he was just finding his footing again. He'd be caught up in her lawsuit and drama and wouldn't be able to devote himself to rebuilding his life. "I think we got swept away with the whole Christmas thing, and I think we bonded on some unfortunate similarities. But let's face it—I'm a workaholic, and I always will be. I'm not looking for a lasting relationship, and you are. You want kids. Marriage. That's not for me. It's easier for the both of us to end this now."

He looked away for a moment. "So that's it? When the going gets tough, you check out? You just run away like this was nothing to you? And yeah, I do want a family. Maybe you don't because of your childhood. Because of your mom. Maybe you're scared to really fall in love with someone and have them really know you. Maybe you're scared that once you completely open up to someone, they'll reject you. But you'll never know if you don't give it a chance."

She inhaled sharply. He...was he right? Her mind raced, combing through their conversations, her confessions, and her need to close off anything that made her feel vulnerable. Until Finn. He was the first person she'd opened up to, and he'd made her feel safe. Was she ever going to find that again? Did it even matter?

She couldn't deal with this now. Not in front of him. "Of course not. I'm allowed to not want commitment. I'm allowed to not want kids. It doesn't matter why."

"You're right. But I also think you're lying to me," he said gently. "And maybe even yourself."

Heat stung her cheeks. "You don't know me well enough to say that."

He ran a hand over his jaw. "And I think that's the most insulting thing of all. I guess you're right—this was nothing. Because if this was something, if I actually meant something to you, you would trust me with whatever you're hiding. You would know that I would believe you, that I would have your back, and that I'd help you. With anything, Mel."

She blinked back tears, trying to hold onto her composure at everything he was telling her and the softness in his voice as he took a step closer. Too close. Any closer and she'd walk right into his arms and trust him like he was telling her to. But she couldn't do that to him. She was a wreck, and she wouldn't drag him down with her. "I have to go. Merry Christmas, Finn."

"Seriously?"

She looked away, her gaze settling on the snow globe. The pit that formed in her stomach was too deep to ever heal. She was making her choice. Her choice was to walk away from people again, people who demanded things of her, people she could hurt. "Good luck with everything, Finn," she said, forcing the words out, even though they were barely a whisper, before opening the door and walking out into the darkness.

Chapter Fifteen

Finn sat in Ben and Molly's living room, holding his niece in his arms, *almost* happy. Full happiness had walked out the door on him two nights ago.

He'd been left reeling. He hadn't seen that coming. It was like Melody had walked into the bedroom as one person and had emerged as someone else. No, not someone else—the person she was before their time together. From what she'd told him, he knew how hard her mother could be on her. It was killing him not knowing what, exactly, the woman had said to upset Mel so badly that she'd walk out on him and all the progress she'd made. They'd been happy those last few days. It *wasn't* fake.

He regretted letting her go without pressing harder for the truth. He hadn't figured out what he was going to do yet, but he couldn't let things end like that. He was going to give Mel her space…and then he was going to find her and try to get through to her.

His niece, Faith, slowly opened her eyes, and peace rushed through him as he watched her try to focus. She let out a deep sigh and closed her eyes again. He looked up at his brother. Even though he looked like he could use a good night's sleep, there was something so confident, so sure, so peaceful that Finn had never seen in him.

"You guys are doing well," Finn said, more a statement than a question.

Ben picked up the cup of coffee Finn had brought over and took a sip. "I know it's cliché, Finn, and it's almost embarrassing to say out loud...but I feel like the luckiest guy in the world. I didn't know it would feel like this. I didn't know that I could love this little baby who I didn't know three days ago like this. And Molly..."

Finn stretched his legs out in front of him and watched in fascination as his brother got all choked up. It was so weird. They were so different. Ben wasn't the guy he was a couple years ago or maybe even just last week.

And why wouldn't he be? Ben *did* have it all. He *was* the luckiest guy in the world. "I'm happy for you guys. You and Molly deserve all the best. And of course, so does little Faith," he said, looking down at the baby.

"Thank you. For everything. I haven't seen Mel yet, but man, she was amazing, Finn. I don't know what we would have done without her and Drew. When she said that the baby was still breech, I nearly lost it. But she knew exactly what to do, and she kept all of us calm and focused."

Finn managed a nod but couldn't speak. No one knew how hard that had been for Melody except him. He had this relationship with her that none of the rest of his family did. She had let him in, and he knew she didn't let people in. But he wasn't enough, because ultimately, she couldn't trust him. And now she was dealing with something all on her own. As much as he thought they'd become close, she hadn't been able to truly trust him with everything. "How's Molly feeling? You guys getting any sleep?" He stuck to the classic new parent questions in the hopes of getting the attention off him. He couldn't talk about Melody right now.

Ben guzzled more of his coffee. "She's good. She's sleeping now. I'm trying to give her as much time to rest as I can when Faith doesn't need to eat. And you know Mom's here non-stop," he said with a laugh.

"Yeah, I'm surprised she's not here now, actually."

Ben leaned back on the sofa. "Because she's at home cooking and will be returning with meals for the next three days, she said."

Finn would have laughed, but he didn't want to wake up Faith. "That's Mom. You, uh, need to sleep or something? I can sit right here if you want and basically not move because holding a baby is about the extent of my experience with babies."

Ben shook his head. "I'm okay. So, what's up with you and Mel?"

Finn stilled. It's not that he was surprised that Ben was asking about Melody…it was just raw. He would have wanted her here with him, visiting Faith. She was torturing herself and depriving herself of a good life because she didn't think she was good enough. "I…uh, haven't seen her in a couple days."

Ben frowned. "What do you mean? I thought you were together. What the hell happened?"

Finn adjusted the blanket around Faith and eased back into the sofa gingerly. He struggled to find the right words, to explain something painful, and not betray Melody's confidence. "She's going through some stuff and walked out. Not that long after you guys left for the hospital."

"Where did she go?"

Finn tensed. "You haven't seen her? She hasn't been by?"

He shook his head. "I know she's texted Molly every day to see how she's doing, but no one has actually seen her."

A pit formed in his stomach. That didn't seem right at all. "I'll get in touch with her and check in."

Ben ran his hands through his hair. "I hope you do, man. Don't let some misunderstanding come between you. Or secrets. Get her to trust you. Years go by, time passes, and you can't get it back."

He knew his brother was speaking from experience. He wouldn't let that happen. "I know."

"Speaking of, when are you taking the physical?"

Finn looked down. For a guy who'd barely gotten any sleep, he had no idea how Ben was so interested in Finn's life. He hadn't wanted to get into this today. But after Mel left, he knew what the right answer was; he knew the path for him. Seeing her reclaim her love for her job had made him realize things, too. It didn't have to be all or nothing. The timeline he'd given himself to get better was self-imposed. Even if he wasn't fully healed in two more months or six more months, it didn't mean that he wouldn't be by next year. And in the meantime, he could pursue this new career direction. It would give him purpose and a goal, and he realized that's what he missed most—even more than being a firefighter, he missed having purpose in his life.

"I can't go back right now, Ben. I'm not ready," he said, hating to tell his brother this right now. Ben was so happy, and they had planned to work side by side until retirement. He might never go back, and he knew his brother wasn't prepared for that.

Ben frowned and folded his arms across his chest. "What are you talking about? You look amazing. I can barely even see that limp anymore. You've made a hell of a recovery."

Finn looked away. "For the average guy. Not for a firefighter. I've been thinking back to that very first physical exam. And all the times on the job that something unexpected would happen during a rescue. I don't know that this leg can be reliable all the time. And all it takes is that one time and I've cost someone their life. Even if I pass the physical, Ben, I know in my gut that my leg isn't the same. It may never be."

His brother shook his head and turned his face, his jaw clenched. "It's not fair. It wasn't supposed to be like this. It was supposed to be the three of us until Dad's retirement."

Finn swallowed past the lump in his throat. "I know. I've come to the realization that I can be more than just a firefighter. I'm lucky I'm alive. I'm lucky I'm well. I need to focus on a future. I can't spend the rest of my life trying to heal a leg that will never be good enough for life and death situations."

Ben stood and shoved his hands in the front pockets of his jeans. "You know I will back you up, whatever you want to do. It's, uh…it's going to take me some time, but that's on me. I will deal with it on my end. You're the best, and I'm going to miss working with you every day. You always had my back and honestly…"

Finn looked away when his brother's voice broke.

"I never forgave myself for your accident. You saved my ass in that fire in the women's shelter. I would not be here if it weren't for you. Same with that little girl. But I wasn't around for you. I was away with Molly when you got injured. If I had been there…"

Finn held up his hand. "It would've happened anyway. Hell. Don't blame yourself. Just stay focused. Because yeah, I won't always be around to save your ass. But I think you'll be fine. And who knows? Maybe in a year from now, I'll be joining you."

Ben nodded. "No pressure. You have to be the one to want it. So, what's the plan? What are you going to do?"

Finn took a deep breath, ready to finally share his plans with the rest of the family.

• • •

Melody walked through the hospital doors, the usual *swoosh* sound that had always filled her with excitement because it meant a day doing something she loved was about to begin, doing nothing for now.

She had made another colossal mistake—Finn. She'd broken his heart, and she'd broken her own. Keeping her head held high, she pushed aside all thoughts of him—or most of her thoughts—and made her way to Cadence's office.

She'd made it back to Shadow Creek in record time only to sit in her home for days, paralyzed with fear. She hadn't seen Molly or the baby; she hadn't come into the hospital. She hadn't reached out to Finn. The best she'd been able to do was check in with her sister via phone. But Addie had texted that morning, and it had jarred Melody back to life. Her sisters knew her so well—and her text, reminding her not to let Mom control their lives anymore, hit home.

It was time to get her life back on track and stop running from her problems.

Stopping outside Cadence's office, she took a deep breath and knocked on the door.

"Come in!" Cadence called out a second later.

Melody straightened her shoulders and walked through the door. Cadence was sitting behind the desk of her large office and smiled at her. An odd greeting to someone who was potentially going to cost the hospital a pile of money. But she'd always been kind and professional. "Hi, thanks for agreeing to see me," Melody said, having a seat when Cadence gestured for her to do so.

"Of course. I was going to arrange an appointment, but you beat me to it. Did you have a nice holiday, Melody?"

Melody forced a smile, even though her nerves were starting to kick in. She didn't know how she was going to handle being told that she was being sued. Shame was already making it hard for her to breathe. She pulled her scarf from around her neck and took her coat off, seeking relief. She was going to have to make small talk and at least appear like she wasn't falling apart. "Yes. Did you manage to take some time off as well?"

"A little bit. Let's get right to the point, Melody. I told you to take two weeks off because I thought you needed a mental health break. I don't have another doctor on staff who takes as many shifts as you do. I know what happened with the Lawry baby took an emotional toll on you, and I wanted you to be able to process what had happened without the pressure of work as well," she said, folding her hands on her desk and leaning forward. Her voice was soft and filled with compassion.

Melody cleared her throat. "I'm feeling much better now. I really appreciated the time away."

Her eyes sparkled. "I hear you also brought your little niece into the world. Congratulations. I hear Molly is doing great."

Tears stung the back of her eyes. Her niece. She needed to go and visit them. She wanted to share in the joy they were all experiencing. She nodded. "It was definitely a challenging delivery, but it all turned out in the end."

"I'm glad." Her eyes filled with concern. "Listen, since you're here, I want to broach the idea of you getting some help, Melody. I'd like you to start speaking to one of our therapists at the hospital. You know they're always available to our staff. It's not easy dealing with the pressures and the losses we face. You're a human being, and you need to take care of yourself."

Melody clutched her hands together. "This isn't what I expected. I mean, okay. I probably could really benefit from speaking to someone. I tend to put a lot of pressure on myself.

But what about the lawsuit?"

She frowned. "Lawsuit?"

"My mother called and said you had mentioned something about the Lawry family wanting to sue me for what happened," she choked out. Just saying it made her want to throw up.

Her eyes widened. "I would never tell your mother something like that. That would be a complete breach of confidentiality. And it's simply not—" She pursed her lips.

Melody sat completely still, waiting, too afraid to breathe.

"There was a conversation I'd had in the cafeteria with Mary, my assistant, and it was about what we would do in the event of a lawsuit. I used your case as an example." Her eyes narrowed slightly. "Your mother may have overheard that, if she was nearby. But no one is suing you, honey. You did nothing wrong."

Melody covered her face and sank back in her chair, relief flooding her body. "Really? I was beside myself. I was here to tell you that I'd leave the hospital."

Cadence leaned forward. "Oh, Melody, we would hate to lose you. You have been such an invaluable asset to our team. I would have hoped that if you were thinking of leaving, you would have confided in me. I'm here to help you, too."

Melody nodded. "Thank you."

Half an hour later, Melody crossed the hospital parking lot, knowing exactly what she needed to do. An entire weight had been lifted from her shoulders, and she'd been given another chance. She needed to find Finn and tell him she was sorry.

But first, she was going to have make everything right between her and her sisters again.

Chapter Sixteen

"She is the most precious baby ever," Melody said as she held her little niece, Faith. Molly and Addie were sitting across from her. She and Addie had planned to meet at Molly and Ben's this morning and had brought coffees. Melody was bracing herself for questions about Finn, but so far no one had asked anything, so she was just enjoying holding her adorable niece.

"Thanks, we kind of think so, too," Molly said with a laugh.

Melody smiled. Her sister had never looked so happy. Even though she was tired, there was a peace about her, like someone who knew they were living the life they always wanted. There was something so right about all of them like this. All of them except her. She had run away from the one right thing in her life. Somehow Molly and Addie had managed to overcome their past issues and childhoods, but she was still stuck spiraling back into old ways of thinking.

"So, how's Finn?" Addie asked, taking a sip of coffee.

Melody glanced at her watch. "Well, that took all of five

minutes of small talk."

"You have *no idea* how much self-control it took to wait five minutes!"

"It's true," Molly added. "We strategized before you came over and decided five minutes was the appropriate amount of time so that you wouldn't feel ambushed. He was here this morning. He looked very...sad. Kind of like you," Molly said.

Melody wanted to roll her eyes but couldn't because her heart squeezed. She avoided their intense stare and decided to look at little Faith, who was sleeping peacefully instead of looking at her sisters. "I'm going to see him after this. So, he's in town?"

Molly shook her head. "He was. But he said he was going back up to the cabin for New Year's. Kind of where we thought you would be. Together."

She bit her lower lip. She'd go there, too. She'd drive anywhere to have another chance with him. It was time she started living the life she really wanted, not the one her mother expected of her. Finn had always believed in her, right from the beginning. When she'd told him about the delivery, he hadn't wavered in his faith in her. When Molly had gone into labor, he'd believed she could deliver the baby.

She'd been wrong in thinking that she would ruin his life. He was strong enough to handle whatever they had coming for them. It wasn't her choice to decide what he could and couldn't handle. He had this unapologetic ferocity that she admired and wanted. And she wanted him. He was the most incredible man she'd ever met.

"Mom called the night Faith was born," she began, and her sisters' eyes went wide. "She told me that I was being sued. I should have told him. But I chickened out. I got so ahead of myself, thinking worst case scenario and not wanting to drag him down with me, so...I took off."

Addie gasped. "Finn would have backed you up, Mel.

Have you spoken to him at all?"

Melody shook her head, averting her gaze. "I screwed up."

"It's not too late, go to him," Molly said.

Melody nodded, not wanting to let them in on how nervous she was suddenly that he would just shut the door in her face. And on New Year's Eve. That would be the worst omen ever. "I will. I'll, um, tie up some loose ends at the hospital and drive up there tomorrow."

Molly nodded. "I'll find out from Ben where he is for sure. You can't start this new year without going after what, or *who*, you want, Mel. Everyone saw the chemistry between you guys the minute we walked into the cabin." She reached out and touched Mel's hand. "Don't let him get away because of old insecurities."

Melody held little Faith a bit closer, basking in the baby's sweetness and in this moment with the four of them. Just a few nights ago, she was panicking that this little baby wouldn't be here. But they were all okay. Now she just needed to make sure she and Finn would be okay.

The next afternoon, Melody marched down Main Street, Shadow Creek, desperate to finish up this one errand before driving up to the cabin to tell Finn how wrong she'd been, how she was ready to start this next chapter of her life—with him.

It was New Year's Eve, and she was desperate to spend it with him. But Molly had called her, sounding awful. Ben had been working the last two nights, and Marjorie was sick, and baby Faith hadn't slept at all. So, she'd asked if Melody could drop of a Luigi's pizza for her and Ben to share for when he got home from work late tonight, when the pizza place would be closed. Melody had gladly agreed—Molly never asked for anything, and it was actually perfect because she could also pick up a pizza for her and Finn on her way up to the cabin.

She buttoned up her coat and gasped as she almost flipped on a patch of ice as she neared Luigi's. She couldn't wait for winter to be over. Though in a few hours, she'd hopefully be cozied up by the warm fire with Finn. A smile on her lips, she pulled the door open to Luigi's, disappointed to see the long line. The aroma of freshly made dough filled her nose, and she pulled out her phone to see if there was any message from Finn. Of course not. Why would he contact her? She'd run away from him like a coward. No more. She was running away from no one.

When she finally made it to the front, she was pleased that her order was all ready.

"Ciao, Bella! It's good to see you! Happy New Year!" Luigi said.

Melody smiled at the older man. He'd always been so friendly and welcoming and had always made her feel special. "Thanks, Luigi, you, too."

"Say hello to Finn for me. I haven't seen him in a while," he said with a wink.

Luigi knew? How did Luigi know she and Finn were… involved? No. Maybe he was just teasing her. She handed him the correct amount of money. "Okay, will do, Luigi." She gathered up the two extra-large meat lover's specials, balancing them carefully because her track record with this pizza wasn't good, and turned around.

And stopped. Now she knew why he'd mentioned Finn. He was standing outside the large window, holding a sign. But she didn't even read it, because she was busy staring at him. Her gaze slowly left his to read the sign.

Mel, Will you go to prom with me?

She almost dropped the pizzas as she slowly walked

through the crowded pizza shop, her heart beating in that way it did whenever he was around. She stepped outside, and he turned to her and lowered the sign, his eyes filled with something she'd never seen before, just for her.

Love.

He gave her a nervous little smile. "I realize I'm over a decade late with this, but I clearly didn't know what I was missing."

The cold wind whipped around them, but she was immune to everything except Finn. He paused as a group of high school–aged girls walked by, one of them saying, "Aren't they too old to be going to prom?"

Melody almost laughed at Finn's disgruntled expression as they passed. She took a step closer to him, still holding the pizzas...and slipped on a patch of snow. In that half second when the pizzas went flying high in the air and she was sure she was going to fall flat on her back, more than likely giving herself a concussion, strong arms reached out to catch her. She held onto Finn as he grabbed her. The pizzas landed on the ground, and he held onto her.

"You caught me," she whispered, still clutching his arms.

He gave her a lopsided grin that told her everything she needed to know. "I will always catch you when you need me to...but you have to let me, Mel," he said, his voice growing serious as he pulled her closer.

"I know. I'll work on it. I'm sorry. I'm sorry I didn't trust you with everything," she said, standing in his arms. "I just didn't want my mistakes to reflect badly on you and your career, whatever it might be."

"You can't decide what I can and can't handle. You don't need to protect me from your life and your mistakes. That's not the way relationships work. I'm here. Let me be here for you. Let me be all in. Let me be the guy who you come to with your problems. I will never turn you away, Mel. Don't ever be ashamed. I know who you are. I know you're an incredible, brilliant, dedicated doctor and a beautiful woman inside and out. I know that from the moment you asked me to prom that you were someone I wanted to know."

"What?" she whispered.

He smiled, a corner of his delicious mouth turning up slightly. "It takes guts to come up to a guy older than you who you barely know and ask him to prom. Even if it was for all the wrong reasons and we shared siblings who just so happened to be in love. Then, when you walked into that cabin, you changed everything for me. Just like when you walked out."

"If you left because you thought you needed to protect me, then that's all wrong. Lasting relationships don't work like that. Good times and bad. You can't hide from me, and I can't hide from you. That's how it works."

She gave a watery laugh. "How the heck did you become such a relationship expert?"

He grinned. "I'm not. But I've learned a lot from my parents. And I've learned a lot of what not to do thanks to Molly and Ben. Though I know they've figured it out now. I don't want to waste time. I don't want to spend my days without you. I don't want to settle for okay. Before you came into my life, I was okay. But when you're in my life, I'm great."

She stared into his blue eyes, knowing he was it for her. Somehow, he'd managed to get to know the real her, the one she was too afraid to be for so long. She has spent her life living for everyone else, worried about what everyone else would think of her. Now she knew that it all started with her own opinion of herself. Who could ever love her when she didn't even love herself? But Finn saw all the good in her, he saw the woman she'd been trying to be her whole life, and he'd shown her that she already existed.

"I want to be great with you," she said softly, meeting him halfway for a kiss.

Epilogue

One Year Later

"Mel, hurry up and shut the door. We need to get this Monopoly game going. Now," Finn said.

Melody frowned at Finn, closing the door behind her. They had just arrived at Molly and Ben's cottage, and Finn was already whipping off his jacket and setting up the Monopoly board on the coffee table.

"What is the rush? We just got here. I want to soak in all the memories. And look, it's already decorated, too. Do you remember decorating the tree last year?" She sighed. A wave of nostalgia gripped her, and she wanted to relish it—something she had started doing this past year. She had learned to slow down. To not race through life like her hair was on fire...or like she was constantly trying to outrun judgment or trying to prove her self-worth. She had worked hard on herself. On letting go of the past in favor of a future she had never thought possible. Therapy had helped. But so had Finn. So had her sisters.

She'd forgiven the girl she used to be and had learned to love herself. She knew a part of that was because of Finn. He loved all parts of her, even the ones that weren't perfect. Her mother's problems were her mother's, and she didn't know where their relationship would go or if there would ever be one, but the anger was gone. She was working hard on pushing aside the thoughts of inadequacy and her mother's voice. She had learned that her mother didn't define who she was. Only Melody was in control of herself.

She looked over at him, knowing she'd found her soul mate in life. There were times before she met Finn where she'd even wondered what kind of a soul she had. But she'd figured it out. He was her best friend. He listened to her, without judgment, whenever she needed to talk—

"Mel, *hurry up*."

She took off her coat. "I don't get what the hurry is. You know I'll win this game in like half an hour. And I'm kinda surprised this is the first thing you want to do after barely seeing each other this week," she said, walking around the sofa.

He shot her a sheepish grin but gestured for her to sit down. She rolled her eyes and sat opposite him, wondering at the panicked look in his gaze. A year ago, she would have assumed something bad was coming. That he'd discovered she wasn't a nice person and was going to end their relationship. Now…*now*, she just figured something was up. She glanced at the tray and frowned. "This isn't our usual—"

But then her heart stopped as she read the various streets on the board.

"It's not," he said thickly.

"Luigi's Pizza…Addie's Bookshop…the fire station…the hospital… Addie and Drew's house…the cabin… Is this a custom-made Monopoly board?"

"Keep reading."

Where Boardwalk should have been was replaced by "Mel and Finn's cabin."

"What is this?" she whispered, her gaze going from the board to his sparkling eyes.

"Pick up the Chance card," he said, pointing to the stack on the board.

Her heart hammered in her chest so loud she was sure he heard. "Finn…"

"I know it's your most detested pile on the board—"

"Nothing good comes from the Chance deck."

"Maybe this time will be different."

She reached across, a faint tremble in her hand as she picked up the card and turned it over to read. She blinked a few times, her breath catching in her throat as she re-read the card.

Advance to Go, Marry Finn.

When she raised her blurry eyes to him, he was kneeling in front of her with a little box in his hand. His own eyes were watery. "Melody, last year you walked in here and proceeded to change my life. We bonded in our mutual misery and mocking of our families but somehow ended up teaching each other so much. You changed me for the better. You made me realize I'm more than a firefighter. And I want to be your husband. I want to be the man who will always have your back, who believes in you, who makes you laugh. I know you said you didn't want all that, but this year…I can't imagine not spending our lives together. Mel, will you marry me?"

She clasped her hands against his face, against the scratchy beard he grew for the holidays, at her request, and looked into his eyes. "You are everything to me, Finn. I love you so much. I finally feel like I'm myself and that I can be myself. You were right. When I said I didn't want any of this, I'd made myself believe it. I didn't believe I could ever trust a person enough to show my true self. I didn't want to burden anyone else. I was wrong. You've helped me see that I am strong. That I can trust others to be there for me. You've given me everything. Of course I'll marry you!"

He kissed her, both of them still on their knees, and then he held her close. She didn't want this moment to end.

The Christmas tree lights twinkled, and as he slipped the diamond ring on her finger, she cried. Because she *could* cry.

Because she had spent a lifetime hiding her tears and insecurities. Because he always made her feel safe and secure. Because he was everything she ever wanted and the emotions were too big to hide. She never had to hide who she really was with Finn.

She looked up from the ring to him. "It's beautiful."

"Are you sure? We can always—"

She kissed him. "It's perfect. Just like you."

He gave her a lopsided grin, his eyes sparkling. "Speaking of how perfect I am, what do you think about us buying that empty lot next to this one? We can have our own cabin. You'll note I did place us on Boardwalk's spot and Ben and Molly on Park Place."

A laugh bubbled up from her chest. "Definitely. You know they're all going to flip out tomorrow when they find out."

He nodded. "I know. We've joined them, Mel. As much as it kills me to admit it, we've become the happy people."

This time, she did laugh as she wrapped her arms around his neck. "A small price to pay."

"Agreed. Merry Christmas, Melody."

And then he kissed her.

About the Author

Victoria James is a romance writer living near Toronto. She is a mother to two young children, one very disorderly feline, and wife to her very own hero.

Victoria attended Queen's University and graduated with a degree in English Literature. She then earned a degree in Interior Design. After the birth of her first child she began pursuing her life-long passion of writing.

Her dream of being a published romance author was realized by Entangled in 2012. Victoria is living her dream—staying home with her children and conjuring up happy endings for her characters.

Victoria would love to hear from her readers! You can visit her at www.victoriajames.ca or Twitter @vicjames101 or send her an email at Victoria@victoriajames.ca.

Also by Victoria James...

CHRISTMAS WITH THE SHERIFF

THE BABY BOMBSHELL

THE DOCTOR'S REDEMPTION

BABY ON THE BAD BOY'S DOORSTEP

THE FIREFIGHTER'S PRETEND FIANCE

A CHRISTMAS MIRACLE FOR THE DOCTOR

THE RANCHER'S SECOND CHANCE

THE BEST MAN'S BABY

A RISK WORTH TAKING

THE DOCTOR'S FAKE FIANCÉE

RESCUED BY THE RANCHER

FALLING FOR THE P.I.

FALLING FOR HER ENEMY

THE REBEL'S RETURN

THE BILLIONAIRE'S CHRISTMAS BABY

THE BILLIONAIRE'S CHRISTMAS PROPOSAL

THE TROUBLE WITH COWBOYS

Find your Bliss with these great releases…

CLAIMING THE DOCTOR'S HEART
a novel by Sean D. Young

When his father is hospitalized, Dr. Eric Bradley must fill in for him as the small-town doctor. Without Holly Ransom, the receptionist, to keep things running smoothly, he wouldn't survive. If only her sweet n' sassy charm were enough to solve all his problems. Eric must leave in a month or he'll lose the opportunity of a lifetime. But how can he leave the woman he's falling in love with and his family legacy behind?

THE MISTLETOE TRAP
a novel by Cindi Madsen

Julie and her best friend Gavin have a relationship that's always been decidedly just friends. Even though their meddling parents have hung mistletoe everywhere this holiday season, Julie and Gavin know some things won't change. Plus, Gavin's the new starting quarterback for the San Antonio Mustangs; he's got enough on his plate without a romance. But when they fall into a "reverse parent trap," their friendship is about to reach a whole new level.

THE KISS LIST
a *Love List* novel by Sonya Weiss

All Haley has ever wanted was her One True Love. Her parents knew they were soul mates at their first kiss, so surely Haley will, too, if she can just kiss each guy on her foolproof Kiss List. Enter Max: bane of Haley's existence but unfortunately, as a local, her way in with the guys. Max wants nothing to do with love or Haley, but the more time they spend together, the clearer it is that there's a paper-thin line between love and hate...

MORE THAN FRIENDS
a *Kendrick Place* novel by Jody Holford

Owen Burnett planned on a quiet, easygoing Christmas, and tells a little white lie to keep it that way. But when his family shows up unexpectedly, he pulls the best friend card to ask Gabby to play his fake girlfriend. Gabby's been hopelessly in love with Owen for what feels like forever, but playing his "fake" girlfriend when the entire boisterous Burnett clan visits is easier said than done. Their chemistry might be obvious, but putting their friendship on the line is a risk she can't take.

Manufactured by Amazon.ca
Bolton, ON